HIGH PLAINS COWBOY

Dr. Carl R. Stekelenburg

Trafford rev. 09/06/2011

 www.trafford.com

North America & international
toll-free: 1 888 232 4444 (USA & Canada)
phone: 250 383 6864 ♦ fax: 812 355 4082

About The Author

Dr. Stekelenberg is a former school superintendent. He was blinded in a mistaken identity attack in 1983. He is the author of five previous Trafford books. These are: The Burton Murder and other Short Stories, Blind Date, Gunfight at Dutchman's Well, Canadian Cowgirl and The Senator. This current book was first released in 2005 by Publish America. It is being re-released by Trafford Publishing in August 2012.

Prologue

Zack, the dark haired, dark-eyed handsome "High Plains" cowboy sat on Buck his one-thousand-pound buckskin gelding.

He watched in awe at the ton of power in the two-thousand-pound longhorn bull.

Zack and his father owned a small ranch near Plainview, Texas. They were gathering cattle for the Amari110 auction, but this bull was objecting. So, Zack and hired cowhand Milton were sharing the chore of showing this longhorn who was boss. Zack swung the lariat in a wide circle over his own head. Now, he released it, aiming at this huge longhorn bull's head. But the muscled brute was having no part of it. He jerked away violently. The lariat had dropped on the ground in front of the running snorting bull. Zack saw the bull's right front hoof step into the circle of the rope. He jerked the lariat quickly to trap the animal's right front hoof. Zack spun three quick twists around his saddle horn. Buck, a well-trained cutting horse, dropped his rear haunches, planted all four feet in a stopping brace. To Buck's surprise as well as Zack's, the bull just drug saddle, horse, and rider like hay in a West Texas wind storm.

The saddle's cinch began to give. The cinch stretched and the saddle slid forward to the front legs and withers of the horse. Zack jumped trying to land on his feet, away from Buck. He landed on his feet, but had bruised his leg on the saddle horn as he went off. Then as the cinch buckle flew off, it hit Zack in the back of his head. Everything suddenly went dark and his legs gave way and Zack crumpled to the ground.

Milton couldn't believe what was happening as he rode to Zack's left, about one horse length behind. As the drama was unfolding, Milton too, had thrown his own lariat around the animal's left leg. He started to take a loop around his own saddle horn, but the lariat was jerked from his gloved hands.

Seeing his friend Zack being dragged from his horse by this ton ofmuscle, Milton pulled his Winchester 44 from his saddle boot. Taking aim on the D-huge animal, Milton held his breath as he squeezed the trigger. "Blam" went the rifle. The bullet entered the bull's head at the point where his spine met its skull. The ton of bull dropped and slid on the ground still pull ing the saddle up Buck's back.

Suddenly it was very quiet compared to a few seconds earlier.

Milton ran to Zack. "Are you okay?" he asked as he knelt down by the unconscious Zack. "I just killed your big bad bull and probably cost you the most expensive beef that we were taking to the Amarillo sale." Milton, getting no response, noticed Zack was lying there motionless. Milton then retrieved his bedroll, spread it out and stretched Zack out on it.

Later when Zack began to stir on the blanket, Milton gave a big sigh of relief and repeated his story, to a now conscious Zack.

Zack, rubbing the back of his head responded to Milton. "Thanks for saving my life," he said. "But don't worry, we can have some very tough steaks." Zack laughed and grimaced at the pain in his head.

Not a very good beginning of a frail drive 10 the railhead, Zack thought.

Zack was half lying and half sitting up on his blanket when Charlie Denton, the ranch foreman, rode up. "What happened here? Zack, you look as white as a ghost." Milton then related the story to Charlie.

Charlie said, "You take the drag for a few days. You'll eat some dust, but it's the lightest work that I have."

Charlie went on. "I want you to ride ahead to Amarillo when you feel up to it. 1 need someone to make arrangements for someone at the auction barn to receive our herd." He didn't know what else to do with this injured young man.

Chapter 1

Issac "Zack" Haney, the only son of Alan and Consuelo Haney, was a strong, muscular, lean and handsome young man. His mother of Spanish descent had passed on the dark olive, smooth skin and hair black as night to her son. Zack's mother had died when he was seventeen years old, leaving the handling of the ranch to Zack and their ranch foreman, Charlie Denton.

Charlie's skills as a cattleman had been a guiding force for Zack. Charlie was only a few years older than Zack, but he just seemed to be able do just about anything that involved ranching. Zack, with less experience, displayed those abilities.

Alan Haney had served for nearly seventeen years as a U.S. Marshall under Judge Issac Parker of Fort Smith, Arkansas, who was the law over the Oklahoma Indian Territory. The second judge to be known as the "Hanging Judge." Judge Roy Bean, being the first. Alan Haney had been so impressed with Judge Parker's legal mind that he had named his son Issac after him.

Alan's new role as a widower had brought his career as U.S. Marshall to an end. His only regret was that his wife Consuelo and their daughter would not be there. He would find consolation in getting to know his son, whom he hardly knew.

Chapter 2

"Easy, boy," Zack spoke quietly to his horse as he patted its neck. The arrow barely missed Zack's head. It was so close he felt the feather tip brush his ear. This sudden attack from out of nowhere jolted Zack out of his daydreaming about the lovely Spanish beauty, Theresa Mendoza, that he had met at the auction barn in Amarillo a couple of weeks ago.

He was now on his way back to let his ranch foreman, Charlie, know prior arrangements were not necessary. The cattle just needed to be brought in. It was completely unlike Zack to let his mind wander from the task at hand. But the closeness of the arrow quickly brought his attention back to his surroundings.

Zack dropped to his buckskin gelding's neck as he drove his boot heels into the gelding's flanks. The gelding was earning its reputation for running a strong quarter mile that day. Thank goodness Buck was a well-conformed, well-fed and powerful animal. After a quarter mile run, he was still breathing in regular deep breaths, even though he had begun to lather and his eyes were showing a good deal of white.

Zack's eyes showed a good bit of white, too.

Now, he reined in Buck and turned into a shallow draw in the Palo Duro Canyon. There he looked back after turning Buck back to face the way they had just come, pulling his 44-Colt revolver from its holster as he dismounted.

Looking over the edge of the draw, he saw the three approaching Indians.

Realizing the Indians were too far away for a pistol shot, Zack replaced his revolver in its holster and pulled his Winchester 44 from the saddle boot. The noonday sun reflected off the gleaming blued barrel.

Finding himself in this predicament, he wondered at the wisdom of leaving the cattle drive alone. Maybe he should have had Charlie send Milton or Shorty with him. It probably would have helped if his mind had been tuned to the things that were going on around him instead of day dreaming about the young woman he had only just met.

The Indians had split into three different directional approaches at the sight of his gleaming rifle ban-el. Right, left and center, they headed to his wash in the high plains of West Texas.

Zack lay in the draw and watched from under his black, flat crowned hat.

Still he squinted from the glare of the noon day sun. His buckskin long sleeve shirt was sticking to his back with sweat. His dark brown chaps were hot too.

His canteen was still on his saddle horn. He needed a taste of water for his parched throat and lips. He judged that he had time to get to Buck down further in the draw. Buck had a black mane and tail as well as a dark black line down his spine. He was a true "line-back dun." Buck was low enough in the draw to be below rifle or arrow shot from the approaching trio of Indians.

Zack grabbed the canteen and took a quick swig. Then Buck's wet mane made him take pity on his horse. Thus, he paused to place his hat upside down before Buck. He poured the rest of the contents of the canteen into his hat.

Buck immediately drank it all up. Zack placed his damp hat back on his head.

The remaining few drops of water saturated his hatband as he settled it down low over his red-rimmed eyes.

Zack's tan from all the years on horseback helped him blend into the plains. As the Indians approached nearer they noticed that the previously observed man who matched the coloring of his horse had disappeared. Both man and horse had blended into the purple, tan and pink reflecting off the far wall of Palo Duro Canyon.

The reflecting sun off the canyon walls helped to hide the black hat Zack barely exposed above the rim. As this was the late summer of the year, the canyon floor was covered with lush green grass and full bloomed mesquite trees. This had been the reason they had chosen to drive the herd through the canyon.

As Zack Iitted his rifle over the rim of his hiding place, sunlight again reflected clearly off the barrel. The glint did not go unnoticed by the renegade warriors. They dropped to the sides of their mounts. This shielded them from Zack's bullets. But Zack was no greenhorn. He hated to kill a good horse, but it was their horses or him.

His first shot hit the center Indian's mustang in the center of its red roan chest. Its back legs buckled and it hit the hard ground. Its rider flew headlong into the long grass, leaving him out of sight. Zack noted his current position but turned to the brave on his right. The Winchester tucked tightly into his right shoulder and the barrel rested by its wooden grip in his left hand. He steadied his breathing as he squeezed off his second shot. This bullet struck the blue roan horse in his braided mane. His spine was broken and he too went down immediately. The brave rolled to the right away from his blue and now blood reddened horse on the far side grass.

Zack was pivoting back left for a shot at the third brave when his hat was torn from his head by a bullet from the brave near the mesquites. Zack had reached down to retrieve his hat as Buck examined it for more water, but was disappointed. The brave had shot an army issue rifle he had taken from a dead U.S. Calvary soldier at the Palo Duro Canyon battle back in 1874. Now two years later he used the last of the shells he had found with the rifle on the soldier's dead body. Zack had a bandoleer of shells. His three attackers were running low on ammunition, but they had dead accuracy with their bow and arrows.

However, Zack had no more water and the day was hot. He hoped to get this fight over fast. A waiting game was out of the question. Darkness in several more hours would help the braves.

Better armed with ammunition, Zack nevertheless made a decision to light a shuck out of the area. He pressed his now ruined hat down on his head. It would still hide his eyes from the sun but not the rain.

Zack jumped up on Buck's back on a downhill run over the now dry watercourse. By riding Indian style and clinging to the neck of Buck he remained below the line of vision of the braves.

When he at last sat back up in the saddle, he was a quarter mile away from his attackers. They had not shot at him. He was safe for now.

Zack was glad to be alive. He knew that his appearance was bedraggled because of his hat, dusty chaps and shirt from rolling in the canyon draw.

Now he redirected his thoughts to seeing the beautiful dark-haired, olive skinned and brown-eyed beauty that he had met recently when he had ridden into Amarillo. He must have been excited at the prospect of seeing her again, why else would he have left the protection of the Palo Duro Canyon draws?

! guess I assumed that the Palo Duro Canyon fight two years ago in 1874 had been renowned to be the last great Indian fight in Texas. I thought they had all been pushed back to the Indian nation across the Red River.

Well, I was too excited about seeing Theresa again to consider some renegade holdouts must have returned from the reservation in Oklahoma!

Zack realized. *Still if a man can't ride to see a beautiful woman, then the West is stil/mighty wild,* he mused.

So, on Zack rode from Palo Duro Canyon to meet up with the rest of the crew. He figured they had probably gotten the herd about halfway between Plainview and Amarillo.

Zack reached the herd at dusk. The Bar-Six crew was just settling the herd in for the night and Shorty was on his way to take the first watch.

"Hey, now that the works all done, look who shows up. It's lover boy."

Shorty smiled a humorous greeting to Zack.

"So, as you lazy short men were resting, we tall fighters fought Sioux,

Seminole, Creek, Cherokee and Shawnee warriors," Zack bragged.

"Five tribes?" Shorty responded. "How many warriors did you fight?"

"Just three actually." Zack reddened. "I just mentioned five civilized or supposedly civilized tribes that have been assigned to reservations in the

Oklahoma Indian Territory."

"How do you remember all that stuff?" Shorty questioned "But you can't cOllnt three braves from five tribes?" Shorty questioned.

Shorty smiled. "Didn't those tribes get sent back to the Indian Nation after the battle of Palo Duro Canyon two years ago? Now you say you're Indian fighting? Was 'she' really the Indian?" Shorty kept up the banter.

"No, not Indian. Theresa, a beautiful young woman that I met in Amarillo is of Spanish descent. Plus, J haven't been courting ladies. I've been fighting at least three renegades who apparently left the reservation and returned to south of the Red River here in West Texas." He asked with fervor, "Do you think I made this hole in my hat up?" Zack pulled his hat off and put his index finger through the bullet hole in the crown.

Zack continued. "Shorty, if it were not a waste of good fighting with such a little guy as you, I'd show you how to fight. You probably need the practice," he said, flexing his bulging right arm as he shook his right fist at the smaller man. Then he turned to help the crew to get the last longhorns in a milling circle. At the end he and Shorty pushed the last steer in together.

Before shaking hands, they smiled and dusted off their hands on their pants.

The crew knew they were friends.

The two friends parted and Zack headed for the chuck wagon sitting nearby on the grass. The other members of the Bar-Six crew greeted him.

"We did all the work, and then fixed the coffee and a meal, not to mention the fire for heating up everything. Now look who shows up just in time to eat,"

Charlie said.

"Charlie, I have fought Indians and helped get the herd in a circle. You left the ones too ornery for your ladies to handle," Zack replied.

"Ladies? You always have ladies on your mind," Milton said.

"That's for sure," Charlie rejoined. "Zack, you good-looking types are never half as interesting to the women as we true working cowhands are," he teased.

"Now for all the credit 1get for being a ladies man, 1haven't seen a woman in three weeks on the trail. Three weeks ago 1 rode ahead to locate the Amarillo auction barn. There 1did meet one lovely lady, Theresa Mendoza.

I haven't had a chance to court her yet!" Zack responded in good humor.

"When 1sent you to find the auction barn, you're trying to tell us that you didn't do any courting," Charlie Denton teased.

"1 had my pick of ladies. Charleen flirted but as she was short, I saved her for Shorty. Lettie was lovely, so 1 saved her for you, Charlie. Kate was magnificent, so 1 saved her for you, Milton. I saved the best, Theresa, for myself," Zack bantered.

"Now if you will excuse me, I'm ready for some grub." Zack smiled, picked up his plate and found a spot to sit.

Chapter 3

Three weeks earlier, Theresa in her split riding skirt had tossed her raven black hair back from her pretty olive-skinned face. With brown eyes set firmly on the job at hand, she helped move some of the just-auctioned cattle out of the bidding pens. She had wound her way down the aisles. Every cow puncher in the place watched those graceful hips and legs move as she pushed cattle with the coil of rope in her right hand. But when she mounted the steps to the auctioneer's table, Zack's heart nearly stopped. "Wow!" was the only comment he could make to himself.

After seeing Theresa, Zack decided to try to win her for himself.

Zack looked good. Big, tall, sun-tanned, freshly shaven and hair recently trimmed at the barbershop. He even took a five cent hot bath. His clean scent preceded him as he approached Theresa at the end of the sale day at the sales barn. Zack was so taken with her shapely body and beautiful face that he could only say, "I'm Zack Haney," when he finally regained his voice.

"I'm looking to sell some cattle when our herd arrives in about two to three weeks," he smiled. "Are you the lady I talk to set up the sale?" he inquired.

"No, I'm not," she responded and Zack's heart fell.

But it recovered when she continued, "You don't have to make prior arrangements, just bring them in."

"But, what if I want to see you again, who should I ask for?" he continued.

"I'm Theresa Mendoza," she smiled and seemed pleased at Zack's attentions. "I'm here every sale day, Monday through Saturday, preparing the payout checks. So, ask for me after the sale of your stock. I'll get your check, and then bring it back to you. Do you personally own the cattle or are you just one of the hired cowhands?" she queried.

Zack wondered at her question. *Would it make a difference if l did or did not?* He gulped and responded. "I'm just working on the Bar-Six crew now, but hope to get my own spread one day." He said in the hope of being an acceptable young man for courting.

"Then the check is to be made out to the Bar-Six?" she continued.

Well, maybe she is I1 't just looking for a rich man after all. Zack felt better thinking that. He then said, "Actually, I am half-owner of the Bar-Six. My dad owns the other half."

"Then, why didn't you say that when I asked?" Theresa asked.

"Well," Zack responded, "when you asked, I didn't know ifit would make a difference if I wanted to see you again."

Theresa's response to him was to whirl around and walk away from him.

017, shoot. I can't let her get away. I guess I had been just plain stupid

Rushing forward, Zack asked her to please stop.

"l owe you an apology, Miss Mendoza. 1had no reason to believe that you had an ulterior motive when I answered your question. Please, can you forgive me? I sure would like to see you when we get back here with the cattle.

That is, if you don't already have a steady beau."

"Okay, Mr. Zack Haney, apology accepted. There is no steady beau," she said.

Then she said, "This Fourth of July is a special Independence Day. It marks the centennial, or one hundred years of our nation's freedom from England." Theresa stared into his dark eyes with her brown ones. "You should be back in time for any event, such as speeches, band concert and picnic. You can look for me on the town square. Also, if you would like, 1can introduce you and the other hands to some of my friends," she said, while looking unblinkingly into his eyes.

"No," Zack replied. Theresa's heart sank, but began to beat wildly when he said. "1 don't want to meet your friends, I want to get to know you better."

He grinned, displaying a set of pearl white teeth to Theresa. "Your friends could be introduced to my friends of the Bar-Six crew though."

Theresa returned his warm smile with a dazzling white smile of her own.

Boy. those red lips need kissing, Zack thought. But he didn't want to scare or offend her. So he restrained his impulse to give her a kiss. Instead he said, "Theresa Mendoza, that sounds great. l' II look you up at the sale on July third and set the final plans for the Fourth of July. I look forward to it."

Theresa saw the interest in his eyes and responded, "It was good to meet you, Zack Haney." Her heart was beating so loudly, she wondered if Zack heard it.

He didn't want this conversation to end. But he knew that he couldn't just keep gazing at her lovely face. Not knowing what else to do or say, he extended his hand. Theresa extended hers. As their hands touched, Zack could feel the warmth course through him.

Theresa thought as she took the work hardened hand, *His touch is gentle for a man q(his size.* And she could feel unfamiliar sensations that made her want to be held to his hard lean body.

She blushed at her thoughts and removed her hand from his.

As it turned out, he was nearly killed by three renegade Indians that could have kept him from keeping that date.

But by out-riding his attackers after putting the horses out from under two of them, he did return to Theresa on the third of July.

Chapter 4

Charlie and the crew got the cattle into the sale at the stockyard. After the sale, Charlie paid each of the crew and told them to enjoy the celebrations the next day and to stay out of trouble. Charlie saw Theresa at the sale, and immediately understood Zack's haste to get back to her. She was indeed a lovely young woman.

Zack got all cleaned up and rushed off in the direction of the town-square to look for Theresa. She must have been looking for him as well, so the finding of each other didn't take long. As he approached her, his eyes took in the loveliness of her.

When Zack reached her, Theresa held her hand out to him and brought him into the circle of friends she had been talking with. Blushing a little, she said to her friends. "This is Zack Haney."

Zack said hello to the group, then turned to Theresa. "I would be glad to introduce you to a few of my cowhand friends if you like."

She responded pleasantly enough with a "No!"

Zack stopped abruptly and turned to look at her. As they stood there looking at one another, it finally occurred to Zack that had been his response to her and he began to laugh. He could already see this beauty was going to be someone to reckon with. When all introductions had been made, Zack and Theresa excused themselves and moved towards a quieter area.

"After the preacher asks the Lord's blessing on the food, we can pick out a spot at one of those picnic tables and have lunch," she offered.

"Great." Zack smiled broadly.

Upon the speakers and band platform, Reverend Grady offered the prayer for the celebrations lunch. "Lord, we give you thanks for our many blessings, including this meal we are about to receive. Lord, we are especially thankful that we live in this nation of freedom now one hundred years old today. In Christ's name we pray, Amen."

He had intended to sit down as had the planning committee, however when Reverend Grady looked at the large group assembled before him, he couldn't resist a chance at a sermon. So he said, "In the second book of the

Bible, Exodus, the Lord gave us these Ten Commandments. As we start our second century as a free people it is good that we remember God's Laws as well as the laws of our nation. Here are God's commandments written in stone.

"Thou shalt not have no other God before me. I am the Lord thy God.

"Thou shalt not make unto thee any graven images.

"Thou shalt not take the name of the Lord thy God in vain.

"Remember the Sabbath day, keep it holy.

"Honor thy mother and thy father.

"Thou shalt not kill.

"Thou shalt not commit adultery

"Thou shalt not steal

"Thou shalt not bear false witness against thy neighbor.

"Thou shalt not covert thy neighbor's house."

In a land with few women out here in West Texas, many of the men began to feel uncomfortable and started walking away from the speakers' platform and moving toward the meal spread out on long tables. Taking the hint,

Reverend Grady concluded.

"May the Lord bless the reading of His word. Amen."

Following the preacher's extraneous sermon, Zack readily agreed when Theresa asked if he would like to eat instead of listening to a run-away preacher that had forgotten he was only to ask the blessing.

Zack's rare combination of handsome face, gleaming teeth, freshly shaven, tanned face and strong, sleek build made him a target for other women as well. So, as Zack sat where Theresa had indicated and that would leave her space beside him, one of her friends, Linda Haley, quickly grabbed the spot next to Zack. Theresa standing embarrassingly alone at Zack's shoulder placed one hand on that shoulder in an attempt to stake out as her claim on this handsome man. But Linda was oblivious to anything but the handsome cowboy just in from the high plains of West Texas.

"What's your name, good looking?" Linda cooed. Then she batted her green eyes at him as she brushed her long red hair out between her fingers.

Zack responded by saying, "Theresa, your friend has taken your seat. If you sit directly across the table from me, I can see you better than if you were next to me."

Turning back to Linda, Zack replied, "I'm Zack Haney." He looked at her green eyes for the first time. *Dazzling green eyes with that reddish hair, she was a desirable woman to look upon. But I'm thinking that Theresa is the more beautiful person inside and out,* Zack mused. Then he continued,

"Theresa, if! would not crowd you too much I'll join you over there on that side. Zack had seen her crestfallen look, but now she was smiling at his offer.

Tension of the moment was broken when Milton appeared out of the crowd. Zack had just moved over by Theresa when Milton slid into the now vacated seat next to Linda. "Is this seat taken, beautiful lady?" Milton inquired.

Linda said, "I was holding it especially for you. What is your name?"

Theresa said, "Linda, please meet Zack's friend, Milton Nelson. Milton, this is my friend Linda Haley."

Zack said, "Let's eat, I'm hungry."

Milton, looking at Linda, said, "Linda, it's nice to meet you."

She brushed his arm with her hand and said, "My! Are all of you cowboys so strong?"

"No," said Milton. "Zack and I are the two strongest of the Bar-Six men.

Modestly speaking, we can rope, throw and brand a heifer before she knows it."

He grinned at Linda and said with a provocative laugh, "Why, if we set our eyes on a lovely lady, she could be wearing our brand before she knew it."

She turned away and thought, *WI!.v does Theresa get the best looking guys?*

Linda asked, "Milton, isn't that beard hot for July?" Then to soften any insult, she continued, "A girl could get scratched up trying to get to a man's lips to kiss through all that face hair." She looked innocently at Milton and winked at Zack.

However, the wink was wasted on Zack. He was watching Theresa's eyes at that moment.

"Did you say there would be music and dancing about dark?" Zack asked

Theresa.

"Yes, it should be cooled down some by then. Mr. Carter plays the fiddle and Mr. Jones plays the mandolin, it will be fun. Do you like to dance, Zack?"

Theresa asked.

"I don't know, I've never tried," Zack said. "But if! get to hold a certain lovely lady close, I'd give it a try." And he did later in the evening as a square dance was called.

But in Theresa's eyes, the trouble was, Zack held every woman in the four couple square. Linda, Lettie, Kate and Theresa all felt Zack's strong arms around them. Theresa was ashamed of how possessive she sounded to herself about Zack when the square dance caller said, "Okay, spin your partner on to the next gentleman, then promenade your new gal."

Theresa ended up with heavily bearded Milton. *Linda was right. He could use a shave and a haircut,* Theresa thought.

Just then the dance broke up with a fight. Milton of the Bar-Six stepped on the boot of a young cowboy from an Amarillo ranch. The cowboy became angry and punched the Bar-Six man. The locals joined in to defend locals.

Bar-Six hands defended Milton's honor. His beard protected his face from several intended punches. lack had tried to stay out of the free-for-all, but when a local ranch hand stepped on his new cordovan boots, his temper too got up. He reached down with his neckerchief and buffed the boot off, but came up with a doubled fist. The punch caught the man squarely under the chin. The local man crumpled to his knees then fell, face first, with his head landing in Theresa's lap.

"New boots, okay?" lack said.

Theresa's hot Spanish temper rose also. "lack, I know that you have on new boots, but was it really necessary to hit the man? The boots can be polished," she said somewhat angrily. She continued on, "My dress can be cleaned as well."

Looking stunned by her comments, Jack could only stare at her.

Regaining his tongue, he retorted back. "Well, I suppose if the man had stepped on your foot, you would have just wanted me to do nothing!"

"If it was an accident, no I would not expect you to do anything." Theresa then arose from her chair, causing the man to fall completely onto the floor.

She then walked away.

Catching up with Theresa, Zack was silent for a few minutes before he attempted to talk to her. She was still looking pretty heated. Jack thought, *Well, here goes. She can either hear me out or not.*

Touching Theresa on the arm, he gently stopped her before she reached another section of seats. "Theresa, you are right. It was a pretty dumb thing for me to punch that cowhand for just stepping on my boot. I guess he really wasn't trying to pick a fight with me and I should have held my temper, so will you accept my apology?"

Theresa looked steadily at him for a moment, smiled and said, "Of course, but I just don't understand why you men have to fight. You gave that poor cowhand a bloody nose, causing blood to get on my dress and on your new shirt. Can being so tough be worth all that?"

Zack continued trying to placate Theresa. "Look, so that I don't foul up the dress size, you'll either have to make it or I'll buy you a dress at the General Store."

"Oh, Zack, that will not be necessary. This whole thing is becoming absurd. Why don't we just forget about it?"

Zack said to Theresa, "Why hasn't some man already grabbed someone as pretty as you are up and married you?"

"Well, there just isn't a lot someone untrained can do in a cow town except maybe work in one of the saloons. I just couldn't bring myself to do that.

Besides, most of the cowboys that come through here are looking for a good time and getting drunk. That kind sure does not appeal to me," was Theresa's reply.

"Zack, yesterday, I overheard you and your ranch foreman talking about you going to Lubbock to sell cattle from your ranch," Theresa said.

"I was not deliberately listening to your conversation, but you and Charlie were standing next to the cattle pens."

"You heard correctly," Zack replied. "Why do you ask?"

Theresa hesitated a moment and then answered, "Well, I'm not so sure that it will be safe for you to go to Lubbock alone. Fighting on our nation's one hundredth birthday is, well-like fighting on Sunday," she said without much real conviction.

"Are you suggesting that I need a chaperone? A man who has fought Indians and been on countless cattle drives? If that is what I heard, would you be interested in the job?" he asked in hopeful anticipation of a positive reply.

"Well, you see, I have wanted to go to Plainview to look for other work, but I don't think that it would be safe to travel alone."

"Theresa, instead of going to Plainview to look for work, would you be interested in coming to the Bar-Six Ranch in Plainview? My dad and I discussed hiring a bookkeeper/housekeeper before I left on this cattle drive.

Do you think that you would be interested in the job?"

"Why, I could not possibly travel all the way to Plainview with you alone.

Besides, I have only just met you and a girl has to protect her reputation," Theresa replied.

"Are you now saying you need to have someone to protect your virtues from me? I wish that you would make up your mind as to who needs protection!" Zack exclaimed.

"Oh, Zack Haney, you know perfectly well what I mean. It just isn't proper for a young, unmarried lady to be traveling alone with a man. So, just get your feelings off of your sleeve," Theresa replied. Adding now with humor in her voice, "You just might be the one needing to have your virtues protected. I have seen how all the girls have been looking at you today. All dreamy eyed."

At this last statement, they both burst out laughing.

Theresa, becoming serious again, said, "1 could ask my cousin Lucinda to accompany me. I think she could go. She is ten years older than I am. But, Zack, that will be way too expensive for you to pay for three train tickets."

"The money isn't a problem. It will be okay for you to ask her along. 1 know that you will like my dad," Zack responded.

"Sounds exciting to me," Theresa said. "I could fix a picnic basket," she added. "What do you think?"

"I think it's great!" was his response. In the heat of the moment they found themselves in each other's arms.

Zack thought. *Oh. what a lovely body you have, Theresa Mendoza.*

Theresa could feel the hot flush rising under her dark cheeks, but remarked as she stepped back from Zack, "I'll just go over to the picnic area where Lucinda is and ask her."

As she neared where Lucinda sat, she motioned for her cousin to come to where she was, a few feet away. Lucinda joined her shortly. Theresa explained what she needed.

Looking a little skeptical, Lucinda inquired, "Are you sure you know what you are doing? You've only known Zack for a short while."

"Lucinda, of course 1 know what I'm doing. Zack is too much of a gentleman to be harmful," Theresa answered. "It will be okay."

"Well, all right, if you say so." Lucinda said a little doubtfully. "I'll have to ask Mother if she will mind Amber for me. I'm sure that she will, but I feel I need to ask her first," Lucinda added.

Zack was waiting patiently when Theresa came back. As patient as a man was capable of being. While waiting, he wondered if perhaps Theresa thought he was moving too fast, but felt she was as interested in him as he was her.

Within five minutes Theresa had returned and announced, "Lucinda is pretty sure she can accompany me on the trip, but she will need to talk to her mother first. When do you plan to leave for Plainview?" Theresa inquired.

"My plans were to be leaving tomorrow, that is, if two ladies can be ready by then," he replied.

"1 'II ride the train as far as Plainview with you. After you and Lucinda are settled in at the ranch, I'll take the train on to Lubbock," Zack said.

"I think that we can be ready," Theresa responded.

"Do you mean that the two of you can pack and be ready to leave by tomorrow?" he grinned. "That being the case, I need to see about getting train tickets," and excused himself from Theresa's company, promising to return soon.

At the train depot he purchased three tickets to Plainview with six silver coins. Their seats were to be just one car back from the dining car.

Theresa had gone over to where Lucinda and some friends were while Zack had gone to see about the tickets.

As he approached the group, Theresa stepped out to meet him. Zack informed her he had gotten the tickets.

"Zack, what time will Lucinda and 1 need to be ready to join you tomorrow?" Theresa inquired.

"Unfortunately, it will have to be early," he replied. "Say, about seven thirty in the morning. 1hope it won't be too much ofa problem for you both."

"Nonsense, we will be packed, ready and waiting when you arrive for us," she answered.

"Theresa, where do 1pick you and your cousin up in the morning? Do you need to let your parents know of your plans?" Zack asked.

"I will send them a letter tomorrow. 1 am staying with Lucinda and her mother, my Aunt Benita, at the house down the street with the blue painted shutters," Theresa said and pointed in the direction of the house.

The dawning of the morning brought with it the excitement usually felt when starting on a trip. Both ladies were ready when Zack called for them.

"Oh, Zack, this is my cousin Lucinda Geoffrey and we are so excited about the trip!"

"Lucinda, it is a pleasure to meet you. Since you two ladies are ready, why don't we leave for the train depot?"

Arriving at the station, there was the usual hustle and bustle. Other passengers trying to get their luggage on the luggage cart, some cowhands loading their horses into the stock cars and conductors loading the mail and packages onto the mail car.

"Ladies, our seats are in the car behind the dining car, so let's go aboard,"

Zack said. "We should be leaving in about thirty minutes," he added.

"My goodness that seems like a long wait," Theresa remarked.

"The train engineer and other train men have to get the coal loaded and fill up with water," Zack answered.

Theresa and Lucinda were both excited about the trip and had hardly slept the night before. Theresa had tossed and turned and this had kept Lucinda awake a good part of the night. Now she hoped that once the train got underway, she would be able to catch a nap. As she began to get settled into her seat, she heard the conductor as he shouted, "All aboard!" lack had rested and slept well the night before. In his hotel room, he went to bed feeling the physical labor he had done recently. His mattress felt soft and he slept comfortably. He now observed the two young ladies as they chatted back and forth. But mostly his mind was on how lovely Theresa looked with the air of excitement about her. Just watching her animation gave him a warm feeling.

As he continued to watch them, he thought, *Can one fall in love so quick(v?* Because he was sure this was what he felt for Theresa. *Love, where in the world did that come from? Why, we hardly know one another.*

Suddenly, Lucinda noticed the way lack was so admiringly watching Theresa. She hoped he wouldn't lead her on and then break her heart.

"Theresa, we are really going in style. Just feel how soft and padded these seats are!" Lucinda exclaimed. lack couldn't help but smile at their excitement.

Theresa said, "lack, you look rested. You must have slept more than I did and your new boots shined up nicely. I must have dark circles under my eyes."

"You look lovely, Theresa," lack returned. "You picked a beautiful dress to wear today." Her dress was of green and white checked gingham and trimmed in white cotton lace with green ribbons running through the lace.

27

Her dark raven hair was tied back with matching ribbon.

Theresa said, "Look at that buggy, Lucinda," and pointed out the window beside Lucinda. It diverted Lucinda's attention as planned. Theresa leaned toward lack on the seat across from her and kissed him right on his mouth.

"Thank you for this nice trip to Plainview. I've never been on a train before, but I have ridden on a steam boat."

Just then the train whistle blew and the train car made a creaking jolt as the train started to move out from the depot. Theresa was thrown a little forward on her seat and lack reached out to steady her.

Lucinda took notice of the way the two clung to one another. As the ride became smoother, she said to them, "I really don't think you two need to cling to each other so. The ride is much smoother now."

"Okay, you spoiled sport," lack responded.

Theresa said, "Lucinda, you don't need to be such a grouch. It isn't like we were doing anything improper. If I had known you were going to be such a fuss budget; I would have picked an aunt, not a cousin to come with me."

"Theresa, 1 certainly did not intend to make you angry," was Lucinda's comeback.

"1 guess that not getting enough sleep last night has made me a little irritable, plus the constant c1ickity, clack of the train wheels going over the rails.

"Perhaps if the train makes a stop before we get to Plainview, you can disembark and stretch your legs and clear your head for a bit," Lucinda commented.

Zack and Theresa talked on a bit before deciding to visit the dining car.

Theresa turned to Lucinda and said, "We are going to the dining car. Do you want to come along?"

"No thanks!" Lucinda replied "It's too hot with the cooking stove. You all go ahead, but remember, I might appear as chaperone at any time." Lucinda giggled.

As they sat drinking coffee, Theresa said, "Lucinda was right. It must be one hundred degrees in here and why did we pick hot coffee'?"

Zack replied, "1 just wanted to have some time alone to talk with you."

"Zack, is there something troubling you?" she asked.

"No, I thought that maybe 1could answer any questions you may have and explain some of the duties that you would be doing. There would be ordering and bill paying as well as running the house. Maybe shopping trips into Plainview for food, etc. 1 said that our ranch is in Plainview. Actually it's halfway between Plainview and Big Springs to the west of Ft. Worth.

Plainview and Big Springs are less busy and safer shopping towns if you happened to be in one or the other alone."

"Hmmm, it sounds like it will be a great job," Theresa replied. "1 was tired of the work at the Amarillo stock yards anyway."

"What is your ranch like? Describe the house and outer buildings please," she enthused.

Nothing made Zack happier than to talk about his ranch. "It's a little east of the tree line. We have greener grass and some scattered trees. 1don't know how much you know about West Texas. Look out the window at the prairie grass. It's browner than our grass at home. There's little water out here. Little water means fewer trees, except near rivers and streams. West of Ft. Worth, Oklahoma City, Oklahoma Territory tribes have made a stock tank or pond as some now call them. They use those stock tanks to break their horses. We have a stream near the ranch house. There is a very shallow end to it that 1use to break horses for our ranch and the Texas Rangers. It isn't much for *d*rinking, but I swim in the deeper part some in the summer. I bathe there too.

"The ranch house has a Spanish appearance. With your Spanish heritage you'll like the arched doorways on this two-story structure. The walls are of adobe. An imaginary line north and south through roughly Ft. Worth and Oklahoma City mark the so-called tree line. Many tribes are east of there and few head west of the line.

"Our ranch is northwest off. Worth but not beyond water and trees. Lots of shady spots near our stream, too."

Theresa sat quietly listening. She had become almost mesmerized by the exciting picture he painted with his words.

"Tell me about the working buildings on your ranch, Zack," Theresa asked.

"We have numerous corrals for working the stock. Our barn holds mostly hay for the cattle. We have small stalls where we keep the horses. The barn matches the adobe on the house. The adobe helps keep the house and the stables cool in the summer and warm in the winter.

"Our kitchen is on the far backside of the house for the same reason. The smokehouse, which is a log building, is directly past the well in the back yard.

We can get water for the house or kitchen in just a few steps. The well pump is new this year. We use one outhouse over by the bunkhouse for the hired help. If you accept our offer you and Lucinda can use the outhouse Dad built for mother when she was alive. Dad and I have a third outhouse down near the stream by the stock tank under the clump of cottonwood trees."

"Have I answered most of your questions he asked.

"Yes, most, except where Lucinda and I will sleep."

"You and Lucinda can use the room that was my mother's. If you decide to stay, then we will convert the room Dad and I use as an office and study.

We will have some bedroom furniture delivered for you. You would be doing the ranch books in there anyway. By the time that I get back from Lubbock, you should have decided if you want to stay or return to Plainview to look for work there," Zack stated.

As Zack and Theresa had left for the dining car, they were unaware that two cowboys seated a few rows behind their seats had been discussing them "You know, Mike, it just might be that there fancy dude is carrying a good amount of money on his self."

Joe's partner Mike responded with, "Some guys think cause they are all duded up, they are the only ones who can get women in fancy clothes. You could be right about his carrying too much money. I think we just need to find out

31

and relieve him of some of it. Why, we just might hit it lucky and get his money and his women, too."

"Let's wait 'til him and that purty woman come back," Joe replied.

A few minutes later Zack and Theresa returned to their seats. Joe and Mike watched them moving up the aisle. Theresa had decided to occupy the seat next to Zack.

Zack announced to the ladies that he was going to take a short nap. He slid down in his seat and pulled his hat over his eyes a little. But he mostly needed some time to think about his part-time ranger job. What would be Theresa's reaction to the news?

The two men moved into the center aisle. They then moved up the pathway towards the seats of Zack and the two women. When they had gotten to where Zack, Theresa and Lucinda were sitting, Joe sidled behind the seat Zack and Theresa were occupying. Mike, his friend, had stopped beside Lucinda's seat.

Joe leaned over the seat where Theresa was sitting and placed his hand on her shoulder as he said, "I could get rid of that dude in them city clothes for you. Then you'd be gett'n yourself a real man." The sour, foul smell of his breathe and clothes wafted into Theresa's nostrils. "Me and Mike could entertain you ladies real good. What do you think, purty little lady?"

Zack pretending to be asleep listened to the exchange through half-opened eyes.

"What I say is you two smelly men just need to leave us be. Why would we want to be in the company of you two with your smelly alcohol breathe and dirty clothes?" Theresa replied.

Angered by the rejection, Joe made the mistake of nudging Theresa. She quickly moved to the seat next to Lucinda to escape Joe's touch. Her sudden movement had given Zack time to react. Zack's left hand quickly found the knife in his left boot top. He decided to avoid gunfire in the car. He never touched his revolver strapped to his right side. Zack rather just followed through with his knife, butt first. The tempered steel handle struck Joe on his right cheekbone. He fell backward in a collapsed heap from the forceful blow.

Mike moved quickly from beside the seat occupied by Theresa and Lucinda.

He stood up to his full five feet ten inches. Before Mike was able to get a blow into Zack's face, Zack's right fist broke most of his front teeth out. He collapsed to his knees in the aisle, holding his bloodied mouth. Meanwhile,

Joe was trying to regain his feet, but Zack landed a direct blow that rendered Joe unconscious.

The two women were speechless at the sudden violence. lack then moved behind his seat, grabbed Joe by the front of his shirt and dragged him out into the aisle and out onto the platform between their car and the one behind. He returned for Mike, who had gotten to his feet and had a dirty looking neckerchief to his mouth. lack grabbed him and shoved him down the aisle to join his friend Joe. Shaking his bloody, knuckled right hand, lack sat down directly in front of Theresa.

"Let me see your hand. It's all bloody," Theresa said.

"Why was all that violence needed with those men? You must be a half head taller and fifty pounds heavier. You didn't give them a fair chance,"

Lucinda rebuffed lack. lack and Theresa looked at Lucinda in utter astonishment.

Theresa had become agetated by Lucinda's remark to lack and had come to his defense. "Lucinda, what is the matter with you? I would think that you would be thankful lack had been here to protect us from those awful men, instead of complaining that he had been unfair to them. After all, there had been two men against one. If Zack had just ignored them, they could have rendered him helpless and there would have been no defense for us. So, I think that you owe lack an apology."

Turning back to Zack, Theresa had said once more, "Let me see your hand!"

"Lucinda," Theresa said, "would you look inside of the picnic basket and get a napkin and wet it, please?"

"Don't feel sorry for those men, Lucinda. They brought the fight to me by their treatment of you two. Furthermore, I am six feet tall and only two hundred pounds, so it was a fair fight. 1learned long ago that you can fight or you can talk and get hit first. 1 prefer to not be the one to receive the first punch. 1fight only in defense of me, my property or my friends," Zack said to Lucinda. lack had added further, "I hope you consider yourself my friend, Lucinda, not just a chaperone for Theresa." lack's comments made Lucinda feel ashamed of her outburst. "Of course I am your friend and I do apologize for seeming so ungrateful," Lucinda replied.

Theresa asked, "lack, I'm your best friend though, aren't I?"

Zack responded to her saying, "Well, yes!"

"However, if I did have a better friend anywhere, do you think that I would tell you after letting you sit there holding my hand and caring for my injuries?" lack added.

Zack didn't like her possessive attitude. They had only kissed briefly one time. *What did women expect? They are puzzling,* he thought. With this thought, he got up, excused himself and headed toward the stockcar of the train to see Buck, his horse.

"Understanding a male is much easier," Zack told his gelding. Forgetting about his injured hand for the moment, he patted Buck's neck and his hand began to bleed and smart again from where Mike's teeth had hit it. Taking his handkerchief from his pocket, he wrapped it around his hand and headed back to the car where Theresa and Lucinda were.

Upon Zack's entering the car, he couldn't believe his eyes. Joe was sitting directly across from Theresa and Lucinda!

Zack heard Theresa telling Joe to leave them alone and that he should go back to his seat, because Zack would soon be back and would be angry to see him back there.

"But, little lady, you ain't never been kissed by a real man," Joe said.

Zack said to Joe, "1 guess the butt of my knife didn't teach you a lesson?

If you want to walk off of this train when it stops, I suggest you stop bothering these ladies and get back to your friend and your own seat."

Scowling darkly at Zack, Joe got up and moved into the aisle saying,

"We'll see you later, cowboy!"

"If you or your friend come back up here, you're not going to need a dentist or barber," Zack said as he brandished his knife in Joe's face. "Now get moving out of here."

"Lucinda, 1 hope the warning 1 gave to him, met with your approval, because I won't be giving him anymore," Zack had said.

Later, the train pulled into Plainview. Alan, Zack's father was there to greet them. "Dad, it's great to see you. Thanks for meeting us here."

Turning back to the train steps, Zack helped Theresa and Lucinda alit.

"Ladies, let me introduce you to my dad, Alan Haney. Dad, this dark-haired beauty is Theresa Mendoza and the other lovely lady is her cousin, Lucinda Geoffrey. Lucinda is here to be Theresa's chaperone."

Both ladies thanked Mr. Haney for meeting them.

"Ladies, it is indeed a pleasure to meet you," responded Alan.

"Theresa, if you and Lucinda will excuse us, Dad and 1will collect your luggage and I will get Buck from the stockcar," Zack said.

"Of course," Theresa responded.

When the two men were out of earshot of the ladies, Alan said to Zack, "There is a message from Captain Brock of the

Texas Rangers." lack questioned, "Did you read it to find out what he wanted?"

"No, you will have to wait until we get to the ranch to find out what he wants," his father answered.

"Well, Dad, what do you think of Theresa?" lack asked. "Do you think she will fill the job of housekeeper/bookkeeper okay?"

"Son, I can see that you have already made up your mind and I can't see any reason why she would not work out," Alan answered.

Grinning at lack, he added, "They are both lookers." lack had given a great deal of thought to his part-time job with the Texas Rangers. This aspect of his life, he had not discussed with Theresa. He hoped that it would not have any adverse affect on their possible relationship. He was sure that he had fallen in love with her. At least, no other woman made him feel the way that she did.

Chapter 5

Previously, Zack had talked with Captain Brock of the Palo Duro Canyon Post. Zack's growing reputation for breaking wild mustangs the gentle, whispering way had long preceded him to the Texas Rangers. Upon his reputation alone, he was offered a job with them.

Captain Brock, of the Palo Duro Post had said, "We sure could use someone like you, Mr. Haney, to gentle some of our green broke mustangs."

Zack responded, "First of all Mr. Haney is my dad. Please call me Zack, sir."

"Well, Zack you will need your own horse and firearms. We provide some rough broke horses as pack animals and spare horses for the outfit.

Ammunition for practice is adequate and that is provided. The rangers have no standard uniform. Therefore, you provide all of your own clothing. Bring an extra changing of clothes and a bedroll. Blankets and towels are provided at base camp here in Palo Duro Canyon. Trail outfits are your responsibility.

Forty dollars per month will be your pay if you decide to join us as a part-time ranger and horse trainer. We prefer single men like you due to the long hours on the trail and the dangers you will encounter. It's better not to leave a widow. Are you interested?" Captain Brock finished.

Zack answered, "I'm interested. However, if! get married later on, would I have to resign?"

"No, we have some married rangers. In general, the single rangers seem to worry less about death and are more daring in pursuit of trouble," he concluded.

"Sounds great," said Zack. "Being part-time, I can still help my dad keep the cattle ranch going? I would love the challenge of training the horses. How many horses would I be breaking?"

"We have about twenty green broke mustangs at the present for a company of eight men, plus me and you, if you join. So, say two spare mounts, government provided horses per man," the captain responded.

"Let me talk to my dad about how we can keep the ranch going without one fulltime hand."

Captain Brock responded, "Thirty dollars per month for part time on-call rangers. Forty for you for the extra horse training work and fifty per month for the men who stay here in camp or on the pursuit trail every day. Leadership roles like mine as head of a ranger outpost pays a little more and no, you can't know my pay," the captain winked.

Later, back at the ranch in Plainview country, Zack discussed the part time ranger offer with his dad.

Alan said, "Zack, I would worry, but if you think that law enforcement would suit you, then don't worry about the ranch. Charlie, Milton and the rest of the men will be here."

Zack answered, "I'm definitely interested in the horse training for sure. I can train the horses here in our stock pond. I've been in fights and gun battles before. I seem to show the other hand during times of crisis. I can see the flight of an arrow or the arch of a thrown knife. I see incoming fists and react quickly. It's dangerous, I know. But someone must keep the bad guys at bay.

Ifno one stands up for justice then we are all in trouble. At six feet and two hundred pounds of work-hardened body, I think I can hold my own," Zack concluded.

"Zack, I've seen you in action. I've seen you work with horses. I know you can do it. I can relate to your feelings from my own experiences with the U.

S. Marshall's job," Alan continued. "Without the Texas Rangers, the Bar-Six Ranch and other ranches would have been stolen blind by rustlers years ago.

We need rangers, so why not, my son?"

Zack beamed. The next morning he mounted Buck and headed out to become a Texas Ranger.

Chapter 6

His attention was brought back to the present as the four of them neared the Bar-Six Ranch.

Theresa could already see that it was all that Zack had described it to be.

Reaching the veranda, Alan halted the buggy. Alan climbed down and then assisted Lucinda.

Zack quickly dismounted so that he could help Theresa from the buggy.

"It is beautiful here!" Theresa exclaimed, as he helped her from the buggy.

"But 1think that were you much too modest, Zack, in your description."

After showing Theresa and Lucinda where they could freshen up, Zack headed for the study to retrieve the message from Captain Brock. These messages only came when he was needed for horse breaking or there was trouble somewhere.

A few minutes had passed and Alan entered the study. "Is there trouble somewhere or more horses that need breaking?" he asked.

Looking up, Zack replied, "They need me to come to the Canyon post as soon as 1can. Seems some men from around Hereford have some new settlers trapped in their wagons. There is some outfit in Hereford that is trying to take over some of the smaller ranches. The greed in some folks is like a festering sore. Captain Brock says in the wire that he only had six rangers in camp that he could send.

"Dad, I'll help you get the luggage inside and then we can see about getting Theresa and Lucinda settled in. Lucinda can move into Mother's old room. Theresa can sleep in my room until a bed and bureau can be brought from Plainview. A bedroom can then be set up here in the study for her, if you have no objections," Zack said.

"That'll be just fine. You just let us worry about the accommodations here. It seems that you have enough to think about," his father answered.

"1 am under the correct assumption that you have not talked with Theresa about your ranger job," Mr. Haney added further.

"No, I didn't. I wanted her to come here so much that I was afraid she wouldn't if she knew that I was a Texas Ranger. I know that I should have told her about it, but that was one time I was truly a coward," Zack responded.

"It appears to me that you have been bowled over by this young woman.

It also appears that you have more than just being a housekeeper and bookkeeper in mind," Mr. Haney remarked.

"Yes, sir, your assumptions are correct on all counts. I just wanted time to court her properly. I think her feelings for me are the same. This problem in Hereford sure is interfering with my hopes of courting her now," Zack said.

Zack added further, "This means that selling cattle in Lubbock will have to be put on hold for awhile. Especially, after 1talked you into buying those Herefords after the cattle sale last year."

"Maybe by the time that 1 get back from this ranger business, Charlie, Milton and the rest of the hands will have them brought up to the pens," Zack added further.

Zack and his dad heard a light tapping on the study door. Alan opened the door to see Theresa and Lucinda standing there looking a little lost.

"Ladies, do come in. Zack and 1 were just discussing the sleeping arrangements for you two. Lucinda, you will move into my late wife's old room and Theresa you will move into Zack's room for the present," Mr. Haney informed them.

Theresa, becoming a little agetated said, "1 can't just take over your room, Zack. 1can share Lucinda's room."

"Of course, she can. There is no need to disrupt Zack from his room,"

Lucinda chimed in.

"Lucinda, why don't I take your things to your room? 1can then show you around the ranch house," Alan interceded. "1 think that Zack has some things that he needs to discuss with Theresa."

Lucinda looking from Zack to Theresa, answered, "1' 11 be glad to join you, Mr. Haney."

Theresa's face was livid. Zack could see the fire in those dark Spanish eyes as Theresa spoke. "Well, Zack, just what kind of arrangements do you have in mind? Did you think that once you got me here, that 1 would just become your sleeping partner as well as your housekeeper and bookkeeper?

Do I look that naive to you? Maybe it is my virtues that need protection after all." Whirling around on her heels, she marched out of the study.

Zack was so shaken by her explosive tirade, that he didn't even try to get a word in to defend himself. *Does she really think that of me? I guess that "Little Spitfire" needs some cooling off.* Racing out of the room, Zack caught up with Theresa before she had time to get to the front door of the house.

Grabbing her by the arm and spinning her into his arms, he kissed her hotly and deeply and then flung her away from him. "Now, you Little Spitfire, you have good reason to have your low opinion of me."

Theresa now with tears streaming down her cheeks stumbled out of the front door.

Alan and Lucinda could hear Theresa's raised voice coming from the study and quickly headed for the stairs to see what was happening. They reached the bottom of the stairs just in time to see Theresa going out of the front door and Zack stomping toward the back door.

Alan called after Zack. "What the blue blazes is going on down here?"

Zack still making determined strides, flung back over his shoulder. "It really doesn't matter. I'm going to get Alamo and Ginger ready to go into Plainview. I'll see you when I get back from Hereford."

His dad still had a stunned look on his face.

Lucinda had caught up with Theresa on the front porch and motioned her to one of the rocking chairs. "Now, get hold of yourself and tell me what is going with you two."

Theresa taking a big gulp of air to try and stop her sobs said between the gulps, "Oh, Lucinda, that Zack Haney is no gentleman after all. He got me here under false pretenses. He not only brought me here to be their housekeeper and bookkeeper, but his sleeping partner as well."

"Oh! Theresa, you must have misunderstood him. Did he say that he expected you to be his sleeping partner?" Lucinda asked Theresa, finally getting control of her emotions, replied, "Well, he didn't just come right out and say it. But it was certainly implied. What else was I to think when he and his dad said that 1could move into his room? Not only that, he came after me and spun me around into arms, kissing me hatefully and then flung me away from him. What would you have thought?"

"First of all, did you even give Zack the opportunity to explain the arrangements with you? If not, then he probably didn't have time to tell you that you would be alone in his room. His father told me that Zack was going to tell you that he was also a part-time Texas Ranger and that he would be leaving later today to go to Ranger Headquarters in Palo Duro Canyon. That is why you were to move into his room until a bed and bureau could be sent from town for you." Lucinda said, more than a little aggravated with her cousin at this moment. "I don't want to be the one to say 1told you so, but I have warned you in the past about that hot temper of yours, Theresa."

"Zack, a Texas Ranger and leaving soon. Well, why should I care? He didn't bother to tell me about being a Texas Ranger when we met in Amarillo" Theresa pouted.

"Theresa Mendoza, 1know that you can be the most stubborn person. You may want to try and find Zack before he leaves and clear this whole silly thing up. As 1said a minute ago, he will be leaving here today and could very easily become mortally injured! In fact, he is readying to leave right now," Lucinda interjected.

"Oh, Lucinda, I have been such an idiot. You're right, 1 do need to find

Zack and apologize. How could 1 have ever thought he would insult me by making such a suggestion?" Theresa said as she went racing through the house calling Zack's name.

However, there was no response. "I just have to find him. I can't let him leave here thinking that 1 had such a low opinion of him." Theresa said to herself and could feel the tears again collecting in her eyes.

Theresa had gone out the back door and was just rounding the corner of the house, when she saw Zack come out of the barn. He stopped to shake hands with his father.

I see that you have decided to leave Buck behind this time and take Alamo and the mare Ginger. You be careful out there son," his dad commented.

Zack then began galloping away, the sound of the horses' hooves were too loud for him to hear Theresa call his name.

Alan, reaching Theresa's side put his arm around her shoulders as the tears flowed from her eyes. "Theresa, my dear child, it will be alright."

Theresa sobbed. "I could never forgive myself if something happened to Zack before I could get his forgiveness."

"Theresa, I' II bet that Zack has already forgiven you. Sometimes we men say things that just don't come out right. Here, take my handkerchief and dry your eyes," Alan said to her.

"Mr. Haney, do you really think he has?" Theresa asked.

"Of course he has, dear girl," Alan answered.

Chapter 7

Zack had been able to get to Plainview in about thirty minutes after leaving the ranch. He decided to go ahead and get his supplies there.

By nightfall he had gotten as far as the northern outskirts of Tulia, Texas.

There he had decided to make camp for the night.

Lying on his bedroll and using his saddle for a pillow, he began to have thoughts of the departure he had envisioned. He could see those sparkling dark eyes of Theresa's and her smiling lips. Lips that he had planned kissing with affection, not the hateful kiss he had left her with. *I should have tried to explain the situation to her. So much for hindsight,* he thought.

Dad has probably explained things to her by now and just maybe, she will have forgiven me by the time I return from Hereford, he further thought.

Zack had not gotten very far out the next morning, when he had to stop and switch mounts, putting Alamo in the lead. Alamo liked to be in the lead, not following behind the mare. "Alamo, you are one troublesome horse. Ginger made no complaints, even though she had to set a steady lope following behind Alamo.

Zack finally reached Canyon after another day's ride. He would be at the Palo Duro Canyon Post within a couple of hours. Alamo cooperated better when he was in the lead. Ginger never gave any trouble in either position.

"Alamo," Zack said to his mount, "you want to be the leader and can't stand being second to a mare. I guess I have those feelings about Theresa becoming more useful to my dad than I can. She can keep house, handle getting supplies at the general store, keep the bills paid, and is probably so popular with my dad for her horse and cattle handling that I'll feel left out."

It hurts to think one can be replaced so easily. Her beauty impressed me, Dad and I'm sure other men for miles around. I better get home to the ranch for courting, frequently, he thought.

Alamo nodded his head "Yes," or so it seemed to Zack. *Did I speak my thoughts out loud?* he wondered. Then he decided the second nodding wasn't a yes answer but a part of the gait Alamo had set.

"Ginger, you're a good girl like Theresa," Zack said. Then his mind was totally on Theresa. He wasn't paying his normal attention to everything around him.

Suddenly, out of a dry ravine Zack saw a rider riding hard towards him.

Zack pulled Alamo to a stop. Ginger stopped smoothly behind and to the left. His supplies for this call up were packed on her back now.

"Zack, Captain Brock says come on as fast as you can to the Canyon Post.

He sent me to speed your pace."

Steve turned his blue roan around and set a full galloping pace back to the Ranger Post. Zack, even with two horses kept pace quite easily.

As the two men and three horses arrived in camp with a dust cloud of their own making, Captain Brock said, "You men were moving! I saw the dust all the way from where Steve caught up to you. Thanks for speeding up. We have some settlers trapped by some cowhands who work for a big cattle spread over near Hereford, I'm told."

Captain Brock continued on, "It's the same old story. The cattle owners not wanting the sodbusters to settle on the open ranges. They have had the run of things so long, they think all this land is theirs. I really think those cowhands were sent out to try and scare them off."

"Six rangers are already headed towards their wagon train. I need you two to bring up more firepower. It is going to be nearly a day's ride. The wagon train is circled up between here and Hereford. Do you have enough food, water, and ammunition, Zack?"

"Yes, I think so. I've packed for a month if necessary. Steve can share some of my pack items on Ginger if he hasn't enough," Zack replied. "I brought plenty of cartridges in my saddle bags and on this bandoleer. Plus about thirty rounds in my cartridge belt," he patted his waist.

"You expecting a war on this assignment?" Captain Brock asked and grinned.

Three hours later, Steve slowed his horse to a walk. "If we hold them at this pace it will leave a cloud of dust announcing our arrival. Maybe a slower pace will save the horses and get us there on time."

"Good idea," Zack said. "Let's water here at that stream."

Steve asked, "Do you have a horse shoe nail puller? My horse's left front shoe seems to be working loose."

"It's in the smaller saddle bag, just in front of the big pack," Zack replied,

"Watch your horse. He's drinking too much all at once in his heated state."

"You're right," Steve replied, "I was paying attention to Ginger's pack and not enough attention to my own mount."

"You can kill a horse with too much cold water, too fast when the animal is heated from a pace like we just made. The loose shoe is probably a result of the pace you were setting, Steve," Zack said dryly. "Use the back end of that nail driver to tap the nail tight again."

"Let's make this our camp. I'll leave Ginger and her packs, then we can move stealthily into the wagons down there." Zack pointed towards the circled wagons half a mile down hill, ahead. The prairie grass was now replaced by trees and greener grass in the valley of the Hereford area in the high plains.

Below and farther ahead, the cowhands circled the wagons. Ranger fire from inside the circle joined with the new settlers to West Texas. Obviously the rangers had been caught inside the circle while stopping to render aid. The gang of cowhands rode down just as the first rangers were dismounted to parlay with the wagon master. They had the rangers pull their horses inside the circle of wagons to give them some protection from the gunfire directed at the wagons by the cowhands.

"Those cowhands are from one of the big cattle spreads," Ranger Shennan commented.

Wagon master Hamrick said, "Just as I thought. New settlers coming out here on the range. They aren't wanting these sodbusters tearing up the range with their farms."

"You know, I think the Lord made all this land to be shared by all men.

There's plenty of room for us all," one broad cloth suited man said.

"You're right, sir, but they just don't want fanners using up the water supplies either," Ranger Shennan remarked.

"My whiskey bottles will soon be shot to pieces if this gunfire continues," one man complained. The saloon I planned to open will be out of business before I get to Hereford. Then who will stop for cards and a drink? Can't you rangers put up more protection?" he queried.

Just then Zack and Steve opened up from the hillside above the wagon train. Zack used his Winchester 44 in a lightning pace. Steve had pulled his second gun from its case under the left side of his saddle as he jumped down from his mount. Zack was first in position behind the log. Steve lay close to Zack's right side. The empty cartridges where hot and piling up fast as Zack pumped lead at the cowhands. Steve repositioned to Zack's left and away from the hot ejected shell casings.

Settling in on his stomach, he manually fed one fifty caliber shell after another into the old Sharps buffalo gun.

Three roars of the buffalo gun to lack's left made him slide away too. The buffalo gun's large rounds landed upon six of the horses and their riders.

With six down, they split into two groups and charged the buffalo gun. "It's a slow reload," shouted the outlaw leader, Melvin. "Rush in while he is loading the next cartridge."

They tried, but met Zack's repeater as they came within its firing range.

The cowboys attack soon broke as lack's relentless firing found arms, legs and hats. Soon the battle was over as the remaining riders retreated. *lack* and Steve mounted and rode into the circle of wagons.

"Thanks for saving my whiskey," said the gambler. "Each of you have a free bottle on me."

"Thanks for the offer, but I'm not a drinking man," said lack.

"No thanks, I don't drink while on duty," Steve said.

"Thanks for saving our lives," said Mary Lou, one of the young ladies from the wagon train. Then she grabbed Steve's arm, pulled him over in the saddle, threw her arm up around his neck and kissed him. She then turned her attention towards lack, intent on rewarding this ranger, too. But lack sidestepped his horse and said, "I don't kiss on duty, sorry!" but he grinned a not unfriendly smile for Mary Lou was a pretty blond.

"Why don't you reward those rangers over here who actually arrived here first," lack said. This pleased Mary Lou and some of the other rangers didn't refuse their rewards. lack only thought of Theresa back on the ranch with his dad and the other men. "I need to get back as soon as Captain Brock says it's okay."

By daylight the next day the wagon train and its eight rangers' escort, started back towards the ranger camp and the town of Canyon.

Palo Duro Canyon was so beautiful that the wagon train stayed to build up the settlement there, which had been reduced in numbers during the renegade Indian uprisings two years earlier in 1874. lack made his farewells with Steve and Captain Brock. Shaking hands, Captain Brock said to lack, "Thanks for coming up to help us out. This post is only manned by Steve, the other six rangers, and me. Sometimes we get stretched pretty thin. It's good to know that we have you to depend on to help us out. You take it easy going back to Plainview."

"Sir, I'm just glad that 1could help out and not lose any lives among the settlers or the cowhands. 1should reach Plainview in a couple of days," lack responded. "Steve, it was a pleasure riding with you."

"Same here, lack," Steve replied.

"Zack, I nearly forgot. I got a poster in just before you got here about a convict, Tony Angelino that has escaped from the State Prison in Waco. The message that came with it said he was last seen heading toward the high plains. Keep an eye open, they say he is bad one."

"Yes, sir. I'll keep at least one eye open at all times," Zack replied.

Zack checked the pack on Ginger one more time and then mounted Alamo. "Well, Alamo, it looks like you are going to be in the lead again today."

Chapter 8

It was late evening when Zack decided to make camp for the night. He gathered up some firewood around the small clearing and prepared to make his evening meal. After clearing away the remains of his meal, he laid his bedroll out near the fire. The clearing was sheltered enough that he would hear any intruders that might come along.

Stretching out on the bedroll, Zack settled in for the night. He lay there on his back looking up at the star-filled sky and began to think about seeing Theresa in only another day. The twinkling of the stars reminded him of the fire in her angry eyes the day he had left. *I sure hope she has forgiven me,* and with this thought, drifted off to sleep.

The early morning light awoke him from a dream-filled night. He lay there a moment thinking of the dark, raven-haired Theresa. Smooth, olive skin that glowed, her young supple body and those soft lips he remembered so well.

The sensation of those thoughts again aroused feelings he had not experienced with any other woman. The warmth of the moment was shattered by the sounds of thunder. Zack tossed back his blanket, stood up and looked at the darkening sky. "I better get this stuff collected up and head for drier ground. Coffee and hardtack will have to wait for later," he said aloud.

Zack reached the small town of Tulia just before the storm broke. He quickly stabled the horses at the livery and crossed the street to the local cafe when the rain began. The late summer rain filled the air with the promise of an early fall. He would need to get to Lubbock soon for the cattle sale.

The widowed owner of the cafe, Mrs. Emma Hart, approached Zack's table. "Hello, Zack. How are you? It's been awhile since you last stopped in.

Guess yours and your Dad's ranch and that ranger job keeps you pretty busy."

"I'm fine, Mrs. Hart. You're right about staying busy. Some days it seems I forget which job I'm supposed to be doing," Zack said.

They both laughed and Mrs. Hart asked what she could get for him. "I'll have some of that hot coffee of yours, biscuits, gravy and ham," he answered.

"Sounds like you haven't eaten in a while," she chuckled.

"Being out on the trail awhile, you get tired of your own cooking," was his reply. "Besides, you know I have to have some of your biscuits and gravy once in awhile," he tacked on.

"Oh, away with you, Zack Haney. I'm too old a woman for you to be trying to charm. I can't believe some sweet young lady hasn't snatched you right up.

I figured that by now you'd have a passel of young'uns." Mrs. Hart laughed.

"I haven't found one that can make a biscuit like you," Zack came back.

Mrs. Emma Hart started for the kitchen saying over her shoulder, "Well, let me see if I can't find you some of those biscuits, gravy and ham, you flatterer you."

Zack finished his meal; paid his ticket and bid Mrs. Hart farewell until the next time he was through Tulia. Stepping out of the door of the cafe, he came face to face with two very familiar faces.

"Well, look'a here, Mike. If it ain't our friend from the train awhile back," Joe said.

"Why, Joe, I do believe yore right," Mike responded. "Joe, I think we ought to pay back a little of what we got on the train, don't you?" Mike added further.

"Apparently that little lesson on the train didn't sink in with you fellows," Zack responded to them as he landed his first blow into Mike's face.

Zack came back quickly, grabbing Joe by the front of his shirt. Zack delivered a blow that bent Joe double. As Joe turned, Zack gave him a kick that sent him sprawling into the muddy street.

By this time, a group of spectators from the cafe had gathered on the walkway. Mrs. Hart said to Zack, "Looks like you made quick work of those two. Do you know them?" she asked.

Yes, ma'am, We had a run in on the train to Plainview awhile back. Guess the two of them are still holding a grudge," Zack answered.

Mrs. Hart looked around, saying, "Why don't one of you men go fetch Sheriff Hines from the jail?"

Sheriff Tom Hines shortly arrived. "Well, Zack what goes on here?" the sheriff asked.

"They're just a couple of grudge holders," Zack replied. "Tom, why don't you lock them up for a day or two. Maybe they will have cooled off by them," he further stated.

So, Zack excused himself from the crowd and went to toward the livery to get Alamo and Ginger.

"Come on you two, let's go down to the jail. I guess you boys didn't know with who you were dealing. Zack Haney isn't only a rancher, he is also a Texas Ranger," Sheriff Hines said to Joe and Mike.

Zack said thanks to the liveryman, mounted Alamo, with Ginger again trailing behind as the packhorse.

The knuckles of both Zack's hand smarted. The skin had been broken.

Guess 1should have put them in some cold water before leaving Tulia, Zack thought.

Chapter 9

Back at the Bar-Six, things were also happening. Linda Haley, Theresa's friend from Amarillo had shown up at the ranch unannounced. "Linda, what on earth are you doing here and how-?" Theresa asked in complete surprise, letting her voice trail off.

"Oh, I guess that I never told you about my Uncle Amos Tidwell that lives on a spread just west of the Bar-Six. It is maybe a twenty-minute ride from here. I borrowed a couple of his mules and a wagon and drove myself over here," Linda responded.

"Well, I can't recall that you ever have mentioned an uncle," Theresa came back.

"Really, he is my mother's uncle. I suggested that perhaps this would be a good time to visit him. Things were so quiet in Amarillo," Linda stated.

"Lucinda," Theresa said as Lucinda came to investigate the voices. "We have a surprise visitor.

"Why, hello, Linda. What on earth are you doing down here in Plainview?' Lucinda queried.

"It was so boring in Amarillo after you and Theresa left. All the cowhands had gone back to their ranches as well," Linda replied.

"Well, are you ladies going to invite me in? I brought you all a basket of fresh vegetables and freshly baked blackberry pie," Linda informed them.

"Please forgive our rudeness, we were so surprised to see you. Please, do come in. Mr. Haney, Zack's father will be coming in soon for his supper," Theresa stated. "You will be joining us?" she queried further.

"We I-I, I don't want to put any extra work on you, but it would be good to share a meal with you and Lucinda. Uncle Amos is kind of old and set in his ways," Linda answered.

"It is no extra trouble, Linda, we would love to have you," Theresa responded and she looked at Lucinda.

"Yes, of course, you must join us," Lucinda added.

"Theresa, you mentioned Mr. Haney, but not Zack. Where is he, you fortunate girl? You always did catch the eyes of the good looking ones," Linda coyly stated.

"How did you not know that Zack and his family lived here, Linda?" Lucinda asked.

"I only came here a couple of times with my mama when 1wasjust a bitsy little girl," Linda answered. "My mama and 1 were talking one day after you two left Amarillo to come down to Plainview. Well, she said she thought that maybe Haney was the name of the people that owned a ranch just a short ways from Uncle Amos. You will never guess how surprised 1was. So, we decided that 1 could come to visit Uncle Amos and 1 could visit with friends at the same time," Linda added.

The sound of someone entering the house caused all three of the young ladies to turn in the direction of the back of the house as Alan Haney entered.

Looking up, he encountered a set of sparkling green eyes looking at him.

Alan said, "I see that you ladies have a guest."

Linda thought to herself, *This handsome man, must surely be Zack's father.*

"No,1 mean yes," Theresa confusingly answered. "This, Mr. Haney, is my and Lucinda's friend from Amarillo, Miss Linda Haley," Theresa stated.

Extending his hand, he welcomed Linda.

Lucinda could contain herself no longer. "Linda has come for awhile to visit her uncle, Mr. Amos Tidwell. She says that he lives about twenty minutes from here."

"Yes, of course, 1know Mr. Tidwell. However, he never mentioned that he had such a lovely niece," Alan commented.

"I do hope that I have not caused a great inconvenience to anyone," Linda said sweetly.

"No, of course you haven't. Please feel free to stay as long as you like," Alan replied. He couldn't help but notice the disconcerted looks of Lucinda and Theresa.

"Mr. Haney, if you and Linda will excuse Lucinda and I, we'll just see to getting the evening meal on the table," Theresa said.

"Don't treat me like a guest, let me help you." Linda spoke up, knowing that was the last thing she wanted to do.

"You just stay there and get acquainted with Mr. Haney, Linda. We can manage," Theresa said over her shoulder.

When Lucinda and Theresa reached the kitchen, Lucinda said, "Can you believe the nerve of her just showing up out of the blue and acting so innocent. I bet she will have things stirred up here good by the time she leaves."

"Well, maybe she really is here just for a short visit. Anyway, let's try to give her the benefit of the doubt," Theresa said to Lucinda.

"Umph!" was Lucinda's only reply. *I don't care how short or long her visit is, as long as she doesn't try to get Alan's attention.* she said to herself.

Chapter 10

During the time that Zack has been away with the rangers, Lucinda and Alan seemed to have become very enamoured with one another. Early one morning after Zack had left; Alan had asked Lucinda, "How would you like to go for a buggy ride with me this morning?"

Stammering, Lucinda replied, "Th-a-t would be wonderful, Mr. Haney."

"Good, I'll meet you out front right after breakfast," Alan said.

Theresa standing nearby, looked at her cousin, who was blushing a bright red. "Well?" Theresa asked.

"Well, what?" Lucinda came back.

Theresa then asked, "Lucinda, is there something going on here that you have not told me about?"

"Just because Mr. Haney has asked me to accompany him, doesn't have to mean there is something going on. However, he is a very handsome man. In fact, maybe an older version of Zack," Lucinda quipped.

Theresa remarked, "Mr. Haney has been alone these last five years since his wife died. Maybe you will be the one to capture his lonely heart."

"Oh, don't be silly, Theresa." Lucinda said. "But . . . do you really think that could be possible?"

Theresa could only look at her cousin and laugh.

Both women began to clear away the remains of the morning meal.

Halfway through, Alan returned.

"Miss Lucinda, as you can see, I am a man of my word. The buggy awaits you out front. If you are ready, we can be going," Alan announced.

"We are nearly finished here if you can give me just a minute or two," Lucinda replied.

"Nonsense, Lucinda. You go ahead with Mr. Haney. I can finish up here in no time at all," Theresa urged her cousin.

"Well, I guess that means that I am ready after all to join you, Mr. Haney,"

Lucinda remarked.

"Good, 1 would like to show you some of the outlying areas of the ranch.

We sometimes have to gather strays from those areas at market time.

Especially, mothers and their new calves," Alan informed her.

Alan and Lucinda had reached the outside of the house and he helped her into the open buggy. Lucinda was as nervous as a young schoolgirl.

The silence seemed to stretch between them and Lucinda could stand the awkwardness no longer. As she began to speak, so did Alan. She said, "I'm sorry, you go ahead, Mr. Haney."

"Oh, no. Ladies first," Alan motioned with his hand "First of all, Miss Lucinda, please call me Alan," he requested. "1 do believe that we have known one another long enough and are mature enough to not be so formal."

"Then, please address me simply as Lucinda."

"Alan, seem to remember that Zack said you were a United States Marshall before your wife died. Is that correct?" Lucinda inquired.

"Yes. 1worked under the Oklahoma Territorial Judge Issac Parker of Fort Smith, Arkansas. He was a very learned man and I admired him greatly. In fact, from that admiration, I named Zack after him. He was the law over the Oklahoma Territory. However, over the years I grew anxious about all of the hangings. You see, Judge Parker, like Judge Roy Bean had become known as a 'Hanging Judge'," Alan commented.

"My wife and son with the help of Charlie Denton, our foreman, and the rest of the ranch hands ran the Bar-Six. While I was gone, Zack was becoming a good rancher under the tutelage of Charlie. Then five years ago, my wife died in childbirth. It was a late in life pregnancy. We were both hoping that it would be a girl, which it was, but 1 lost them both." Then Alan fell silent.

"Alan, 1am so sorry. It must have been very hard on you," Lucinda said and she put her hand over his.

"Enough said from this old man."

Alan then turned in the direction of Lucinda and said, "Then I met this lovely young woman named Lucinda and she is the first woman in all this time to stir the longings of this old man. Longings that 1 felt I would never experience again," he said.

Lucinda was speechless at his words. Clearing her throat, she said, "Those are the most complimentary words 1 have ever heard, Alan. Thank you. But there is something that 1 must tell you about myself.

"I was previously married and out of that union I had a little girl, who is now five years old and her name is Amber. My husband died when Amber was a year old. So, I too, know the pain of loss, of being lonely and wondering if there could ever be someone that would come along that \\lould want my daughter as well as me. How can you say that you are an old man? You cannot possibly be more than eight or ten years older than I am. You are very handsome and appealing."

Lucinda continued, "The main difference between us is that you have a grown son and I still have a dependent daughter. I hope that by telling you this, that it has not changed your feelings about me."

"So, where is your daughter now?" Alan asked.

"She is with my mother in Amarillo," Lucinda replied.

"Lucinda, what you have told me could never change my feelings for you.

I find you much too charming and desirable," Alan assured her.

By this time, Alan had drawn the buggy to a stop. He then turned in his seat so that he could better see Lucinda's face.

"Alan, I am so lonesome for my daughter. I have never left her for any length of time before. I want her here with me. If that is not possible, then I shall just have to return to Amarillo very soon to relieve my mother of Amber," Lucinda stated a little sternly.

Suddenly, Alan burst out laughing at the stern look on Lucinda's face.

"This is not a laughing matter. I want my daughter to be with me," Lucinda reiterated.

Alan's face became sober and he said, "I was not laughing at you or your request. I was laughing at your determined look. Please accept my apology.

I would love to meet your daughter Amber and bring her here."

Unable to resist her any longer, Alan reached for Lucinda and gently embraced her before placing a feather soft kiss on her lips. Lucinda soon found herself returning his kiss, not wanting it to stop. Still clinging to one another, Lucinda said, "Alan, thank you for allowing Amber to join me and for a most enjoyable morning."

"Lucinda, I have wanted to do that since the first time I saw you step from the train. So, the pleasure has been all mine," Alan said with a warm smile.

Upon returning to the ranch house, Lucinda noticed the mule drawn wagon that Linda had been arriving in every day. She and Theresa were sitting in rocking chairs on the veranda, but at this moment, their presence was hardly noticed by Lucinda. Lucinda felt she was floating on a cloud.

"What in the world is with her?" Linda asked.

"Lucinda and Mr. Haney have just returned from an early morning buggy ride. I would say that she looks as if she is in a daze and she also has the look of a woman who has been thoroughly kissed," Theresa responded to Linda's question.

"Well, if Zack were here, I bet I would have a good time on a buggy ride with him. When is he supposed to be back anyway?" Linda commented and she could see that her comment irritated Theresa.

"Zack is a part-time ranger and he was called away on business. We are not sure of just when he will be back. I just hope that he comes home unharmed," Theresa stated.

Theresa's thoughts returned to the day he had left. *I was so unfair to him, but he had not tried to explain things to me. I guess I really didn't give him a chance. Maybe the Lord will give me a second chance and I sure hope that Zack has forgiven me.*

Chapter 11

Meanwhile, on the way back to Plainview, lack thought, *I'll be reaching Plainview before dark, so I think that I will stop here in Edmondson and have something to eat before riding on. But on second thought, I think that I'll just get a cup of coffee at the Cattleman '.'I Saloon. I really am anxious to get to the Bar-Six and see how dad has been doing while I have been gone on Texas Ranger duty. I want to see how Theresa is working out as housekeeper and bookkeeper.* But in truth he admitted, *I miss her and want to court her right away.*

That '.'I not all that I will be glad of I can hardly wait to get this ornery critter, Alamo back and get Buck again, lack tacked on to his thoughts.

As he neared the Cattleman's Saloon, lack reined Alamo and Ginger in at the livery stable. He asked that both horses be given plenty of hay, oats and water. lack then stepped out into the street and headed toward the saloon.

Inside of the saloon, lack stepped to the right of the batwing doors for his eyes to adjust to the dark interior. "Never stand in the doorway light," he recalled from his ranger training.

Oil lamps were placed on various tables. lack's eyes scanned the room for an empty table when his eyes were drawn to a man that quickly turned down his lamp's wick. *Someone doesn't want his face seen,* was lack's thought.

So, he studied the man's face. It reminded lack of a wanted poster he had seen at the Ranger Post. *By trying to hide, he actually pulled my eyes more in his direction,* lack considered. Then the name on the poster came to him, Tony Angelino. *Could I have found him this easily?* he asked himself.

Tony Angelino had been out running the law ever since his escape from a Waco Prison. lack ordered hot coffee. He watched his man through hooded eyes from under his flat brimmed black hat.

When a young lady approached the man, she pointed towards lack and said, "That man hasn't taken his eyes off of you, Tony, since he came in here." They both looked in Zack's direction.

Tony's eyes met Zack's and Zack knew he was about to face gunfire.

Zack, leaving his chair, arose to the floor as his right hand brought up his revolver. Zack was so fast that Tony replaced his own gun that had not completely left its holster. Tony then placed his hand close to the oil lamp on his table.

Zack kept Tony covered as he moved up to his table. "Ma'am, are you a look out for Tony?" Zack asked pointedly.

"Why don't you rangers just leave an innocent man alone?" Sarah asked with venom in her voice.

"Who said that I was a ranger?" Zack asked.

Tony said, "It's easy to spot you rangers and Sarah had nothing to do with me noticing the way you been watching me. What do you want?" Tony angrily asked.

"It may just be a coincidence, but you look just like Tony Angelino, whose picture I saw on a wanted poster at the Ranger Post in Canyon."

"No way! You're right it is just a coincidence. I'm just minding my own business, not doing anything wrong," Tony replied.

"Then, why did you reach in a threatening way for your side arm?" Zack held his gaze.

Sarah had jumped from her chair when she thought there was about to be gunfire. She then made a sudden move toward Zack. In that split second, Tony tipped the oil lamp over.

The lamp exploded in flames. Tony's eyes were on the flames and Zack put his unawareness to use. Quickly he moved around the flames to put handcuffs on him. Sarah moved behind Zack. He heard the shots as they rang out from a Derringer in Sarah's hand.

One slug hit Zack midway up on his back on the left side near his heart but more in the ribcage and back muscles. Trying to avoid Tony being hurt by Zack, Sarah's other shot hit his left arm on the inside bicep muscle. Luckily no bones were broken and no major arteries or veins were severed and no internal organs were damaged. But Zack was in terrible pain and had lost a fair amount of blood on the floor of the Cattleman's Saloon.

The barkeeper sent another cowboy to fetch Doc White as well as the sheriff.

Tony took that time to leave the saloon with Sarah after she shot Zack.

Sheriff and deputies pursued Tony only as long as there was daylight, then returned to Edmondson.

Doc White temporarily patched Zack up. No blood transfusions or antibiotics were available in 1876. So, Doc took care of Zack the best he could. He had applied whiskey inside of the places where the bullets had been removed. Zack drifted in and out of consciousness the rest of the day.

Early the next morning he was still in no condition to travel, but was determined to get to the Bar-Six and Theresa.

Doc White gave him instructions to clean and change the bandages daily.

Zack assured him that his dad and their housekeeper would see to the bandages at the Bar-Six. Against the advice of Doc White to rest another day, Zack asked that his mount and spare horse be brought to him and through a strong will he mounted Alamo with the help of Doc.

Zack was struggling to stay upright in the saddle by the time he spotted the Spanish-style hacienda he and Alan called home. He was looking for Theresa expectantly when Linda rushed from a rocker to his side. She took hold of him as he half fell from his saddle and she yelled, "Theresa, come quickly."

Both Theresa and Linda had been waiting for Zack to return from Canyon.

The two women guessed what the other was waiting for so a state of sullen truce existed heavily in the Spanish-style ranch house. As a new employee, Theresa wanted to make a good impression on Zack's father. Thus, she resolved to hold her tongue and put up with Linda's daily excuses to be under foot.

Linda was upset that Theresa had gained Zack's attention before she did back in Amarillo. Theresa was her friend, but she was determined to win the affections of Zack, so she tried to make herself useful in a pretentious way.

Theresa had been missing Zack for days. She had hoped that he would be getting home soon, but not in the condition in which he arrived.

"Here, let's get you inside," Theresa took command of the situation.

"Linda, let's try to get him to the sofa," Theresa said.

The two women struggled to get him to the veranda and into the house.

Zack was half-conscious and of little help. Finally getting him to the sofa, they gently lowered him onto it.

"Linda, please see that one of the men finds Alan and Milton right away.

Tell them to come to the house at once. We are going to need help getting Zack up the stairs to his room. Someone will also need to take care of Alamo and Ginger and put them in the corral," she half ordered Linda.

"Yes, ma'am," Linda test responded. She wanted to still be holding Zack but complied to avoid a scene. There would still be time for her to work her wiles with him.

Then Theresa began to unbutton Zack's shirt to further expose the bloodied dressings as she helped him turn onto his side. The blood on the bandages was a bright red, so his wounds had been bleeding recently.

With a breathless sigh, Theresa asked, "Oh, Zack, what on earth happened to you? I need to clean and re-bandage your wounds," she said with calmness in her voice. Calmness she really did not feel.

Lucinda came into the room to investigate the yelling she had heard. She was alarmed at the scene she saw and asked, "What can I do to help you, Theresa?"

"Please get me a blanket," Theresa answered. Then you can help me get this shirt off Zack."

Returning with the blanket, Lucinda asked, "What on earth has happened to Zack?"

"I can't say for sure until 1get these bandages off," Theresa replied.

Zack roused enough to say, "Shot. Twice."

As Linda reentered the living room, Theresa inquired, "Were you able to find someone to locate Alan and Milton?"

"Yes, Milton was in the barn and he has gone to fetch Alan," Linda answered her.

Theresa then turned to Lucinda, "Would you please get some clean bandages?"

"Linda, would you please get some water heating on the stove'?"

Both women replied, "Yes."

Theresa then turned her attention to the task of checking around the wounds. She gingerly lifted the edge of the bandage on the wound inside of Zack's arm. There seemed to be no redness or other evidence of infection.

Rushing into the living room, Alan asked, "What has happened here?"

Theresa responded, "It appears that he has been shot twice, once on the inside of his arm and once high up on his back. The ride back here is probably the reason the bleeding has started. I was about to change the dressings, but since you and Milton are here, he needs to be gotten to his room and into bed."

"Right," Alan replied. "Milton, if you can help me, I think we can get him up the stairs and into his room with no trouble."

The three women followed the men up the stairs and into Zack's room.

Zack then roused again to peer at Theresa's face. The face he had been so anxious to see.

"Alan, if you and Milton will get his boots and pants off and get him in the bed, then I can clean and put new dressings on the wounds."

"Hmm, let me help you," Linda said.

"Linda, I do believe that Alan and Milton can do that without your help," Theresa interjected.

"Theresa, was he able to tell you what happened?" Alan asked.

"Dad," Zack said as he was finally getting his wits about him. "I was in the process of apprehending an escaped convict that I ran onto in Edmondson. As

I tried to put handcuffs on him, his lady friend shot me from behind."

"Well, I am glad that her aim was not more accurate," his father replied.

Zack noticed the "Alan" instead of "your dad" or Mr. Haney and was alarmed. *Was Dad interested in Theresa?* he wondered. *She is beautiful and Dad has been without a woman around since mother died several years back.*

Was Theresa interested in his handsome older father who wasn't awtry on ranger duties? Zack worried himself.

Maybe, he, Zack, would end up without Theresa. Would his father do that, knowing how he felt about Theresa? The thoughts of that happening made him feel a jealous rage. He would have to leave the Bar-Six. He couldn't stay here without her.

"Ladies, if you will just step outside of the room, Mr. Haney and I will get Zack undressed and into bed," Milton informed them.

"Milton, you and Alan are no fun," Linda chided him.

Both Linda and Theresa called Dad Alan! So, maybe I am worrying for nothing, Zack thought.

"Okay, ladies, you can come back in and finish up," Alan said.

"Here," Linda said, "let me get those bandages off." However, her bravado was short lived. The sight of the wounds was too much for her.

"Linda, if you will bring that pan of hot water over here, I can get finished with this task," Theresa said.

"Yes, ma'am," Linda said a bit terse.

Theresa removed the soiled bandage on Zack's back. She and Lucinda made a soft gasping sound at the sight of the wound. Linda again had to turn away. Her movements did not go unnoticed by Theresa, but she continued to redress the wounds without making comment. As she finished up, she said, "Linda, Lucinda and 1are going to take care of these soiled dressings and the water. I will be back shortly."

This suited Linda perfectly. She was determined to remove Theresa from Zack's mind. Hearing Theresa returning, Linda applied generous soft fingertips to Zack's back and arms. She didn't stop there; she also began to place light kisses to the back of his neck. Her touch felt s-o-o wonderful to Zack.

Zack was still not completely awake and now he was nearly breathless from Linda's touches.

Theresa, just coming in the door, saw Linda place a kiss on Zack's back, near his neck. "1 guess that 1 should have knocked before I entered. Perhaps your injuries will be better tended to by Linda in the future, Zack!" Theresa exclaimed angrily. She then hastily retreated from the room.

"Theresa, please listen. This is not what it appears," Zack said in a whispered voice.

Reaching the living room, Theresa sat down in the first chair she came to and began to softly weep. She heard Alan and Milton coming into the house.

She quickly dabbed at her tears just before they reached the living room.

Alan noticed the redness in Theresa's eyes, as did Milton. Neither of them made any comment. "Milton, why don't you go up and see how Zack is doing?" Alan said.

"Sure thing, Mr. Haney," Milton replied.

"Milton, that shouldn't be necessary. Linda seems to be taking care of him quite well," Theresa informed him.

"I think 1 will just peek in anyway," Milton replied to her statement.

Something told him he should have kept a closer eye on Linda.

"Theresa, is there anything that you need to talk to me about?" Alan inquired.

"No, sir," Theresa replied.

"Nonetheless, I want you to know that I am a good listener if you need one," Alan said to her.

"Thank you for your concern," Theresa said.

Zack's bedroom door was slightly ajar and Milton could hear the exchange of words between Linda and Zack.

"Zack, whatever did you mean by it isn't what it appears to be?" Linda questioned Zack.

Zack was trying earnestly to become fully awake. "I think you know what I am talking about, Linda. You are a lovely and desirable woman, but I am in love with Theresa and I thought you were her friend. Also, in case you didn't know it, there is a certain cowhand that cares a great deal about you."

Linda could only look at Zack with an incredulous look. "Well, it would appear that I have made a complete fool of myself. I have come here every day waiting for your return. But all for naught," was her reply.

Milton decided it was time for him to make his entry into the bedroom.

Both Linda and Zack greeted him with a smile.

Teasingly, Milton said, "Linda, I know that you had your heart set on Zack's getting back here in time to take you to the Saturday night dance, but with him laid up, that won't be possible. So, why not go with me or Theresa could go if you are busy tending to Zack."

"Yes, Linda. You had best go with Milton to the dance if you desire an escort," Theresa said as she entered into the room.

"Why, Milton Nelson, I thought that you never would ask me to the dance.

Yes, 1would be delighted to go with you," Linda said cheerfully. "Besides, it appears that Theresa has put her brand on Zack."

Milton's face lit up like a light. He and Linda were talking softly as they left Zack's room together. "Milton, 1do hope that you are planning to clean your face of all that bushy beard? 1can't help but think you are hiding a real handsome face behind all that fuzz."

Milton blushed deeply and replied, "I would do just about anything for you my little green-eyed beauty."

Chapter 12

A couple of days after Zack had gotten home with his injuries; Shorty, one of the ranch hands at the Bar-Six was lonesome for his family ranch in Lamesa. Plainview was too hilly. Also, he had not been able to gain the interest of Linda or Theresa. They both seemed to be competing for Zack.

But, Theresa had been real nice to him. She didn't make any difference between him and the other hands. It didn't seem to matter to her that he was short. So, he figured that was zero for two.

"I best go to the house and wish Zack a quick get well and goodbye," Shorty said to himself.

As he approached Zack's room, he heard Theresa say to Zack, "Is there anything else that you will be needing before I return down stairs'?"

Zack responded, "Theresa, please, I want to talk to you about what you saw the other day. Come here, please. 1need to give you a hug for all that you have done while 1was away on ranger business. Not only do you do all of the housework and bookkeeping, you now have to take care of this injured man as well. Thanks!"

Theresa replied, "I don't believe that you have anything to say that 1want to hear. Now if you will excuse me, I have other chores to attend to. Lucinda nor Linda seem to be available this morning."

"If you are not willing to hear me out, then I guess I don't need anything else," Zack said woefully.

Theresa left his room as Shorty reached the top of the stairs. "Ma'am, is it okay if I go in and talk with Zack'?" Shorty asked.

"Of course," Theresa answered him.

Shorty knocked on Zack's door. Then he said, "Zack, it's Shorty. Can 1 talk to you a minute'?"

Zack answered back, "Come on in, Shorty."

Upon entering the room, Shorty said, "I know that it is short notice, but with the cattle sale over in Amarillo, 1think that your dad, Charlie, Milton and Theresa can handle things now. 1hope you get better real soon and can get to know Theresa better. She is wonderful!" Shorty left the room with that last remark.

"Shorty, you have a safe trip home and I have certainly enjoyed working with you," Zack said to his retreating back.

As Shorty had been about to mount his horse, he saw a stranger approaching the ranch house. "Hey, mister, who are you looking for?" Shorty asked.

Ignoring Shorty completely, Tony Angelino yelled, "Ranger, come on out here. 1know you are not going to stop hunting me until one or both of us is dead."

Getting no response from the stranger, Shorty pulled his gun from its holster. Then, without a word; Tony turned and fired at Shorty. Shorty returned the fire as he went face down in the dust. Shorty was dead.

Theresa had returned to Zack's room to bring his lunch, when she and Zack heard the man yell and then gunfire. Zack knew the voice calling from outside belonged to Tony Angelino.

As Zack reached for his pants, Theresa cried out, "Zack, you are in no condition to leave this room. Please get back in your bed."

"I can't, Theresa. 1 have to see about Shorty. The man outside is Tony Angelino. Now stay here out of the way."

Zack finally reached the stairs after a bit of a struggle. His wounds were still very sore, but he refused to stop. Holding to the staircase banister, he finally reached the bottom of the stairs. He could still hear Tony, yelling for him to come out. As he reached the kitchen he staggered over to the gun rack by the back door, pulling his revolver from its holster. He then went out the back door. His body felt heavier with every step he took. Finally he reached the comer of the ranch house.

"Tony, drop your gun," Zack called.

Whirling in the direction of the voice, Tony fired a shot that cracked the adobe on the comer of the house. Zack had ducked back just in time.

Now, Zack taking careful aim, fired his gun. Tony Angelino dropped to the ground as the bullet from Zack's gun entered the center of his chest. Zack knew he had found the deadly mark.

Sarah, the young woman traveling with Tony came running across the yard to where Tony lay motionless. Dropping down beside him, she let out a scream of despair.

"You killed him, Ranger," and she picked up Tony's gun, aiming it at Zack.

"Ma'am, you knew that it had to come to this. That it had to be me or Tony," Zack replied. "Now please put the gun down."

Sarah called back, "You rotten, Ranger," as she pulled the trigger.

Suddenly the sound of gunfire came from behind Zack. Sarah dropped the gun and lay with her head on Tony's blood soaked chest as she drew her last breath.

Zack slowly turned to see Theresa standing behind him with his Winchester rifle in her hands. Tears streamed from her eyes as she stepped into the safety of Zack's arms.

Zack held her tightly as he assured her that it was all over.

Theresa sobbed. "Oh, Zack, I was so afraid for you." She then began to place wet kisses over his face as she clung to him.

Zack returned her kisses as he murmured, "Theresa Mendoza, 1love you."

Theresa thought her heart would burst with happiness. "Zack Haney, I love you, but we have a few things to talk about."

Charlie and Milton reached the young couple at the same time. Charlie looking worriedly at Zack asked, "Are the two of you okay?"

"Yes, we are, but Shorty didn't make it. He was just leaving after telling me that he had decided to return to his family's ranch in Lamesa. I wish that he would of decided sooner," Zack responded to Charlie.

Linda had just gotten to the Bar-Six and was pulling the mule drawn wagon up beside the barn when Tony came up. Hearing the anger in his voice and seeing him gun down poor Shorty, she had slipped inside of the barn. She felt riveted to the spot when she saw Zack and then Theresa reach the corner of the ranch house. Now that everything seemed to be over, she finally found the nerve to leave the barn. She too, had tears streaming down her face when she reached the others.

"I was so scared. I just couldn't seem to move from inside of the barn. Poor Shorty did not stand a chance against that man," Linda said tearfully.

Milton, seeing her distress, put his arm around her shoulder in a comforting manner.

Zack said to Milton, "Take the buckboard and carry the bodies into the undertaker. Tell him to send Tony's and his lady friend's bodies to the sheriff in Waco. As for Shorty, tell him to bring his body back here in a few days for burial."

Milton turned to go ready the buckboard when he said, "Miss Linda, you come with me, because 1know that I sure can use some company on this trip to town."

Linda was too happy to join him. She needed the comfort of those strong arms.

"Milton, tell the preacher to come out here in a few days to give Shorty a proper burial. Then, later that day, I will have another job for him to perform."

Charlie grinned and said to Milton, "I believe that we are going to have a wedding shortly."

Linda, still clinging to Milton, looked up into his face and said, "A double wedding would be so nice."

"Now look what you have gone and done, Zack. Come on here, woman, we need to get these bodies to town before dark falls," Milton lamented.

Theresa, now supporting Zack asked, "Charlie, can you help me get Zack back upstairs to his room please?"

Zack then spoke up and asked, "Has anyone seen my dad this morning or for that matter, Lucinda also? Is there something going on here that I don't know about?"

Theresa knew what was going on, but she feigned innocence as she looked at Zack.

Charlie spoke up about that time, "I don't want to be one to carry tales, but I have seen the two of them on several mornings leaving the ranch in the buggy. I think that they also went out this morning and haven't come back in."

"I guess that they are old enough to take care of themselves. I have more important things on my mind right now. So, Charlie, if you and Theresa will help me get back to my room and bed, I would appreciate it."

After Charlie had gone from Zack's room, Zack asked Theresa. "How does Shorty know how wonderful you are?"

"Issac Haney, if you think that I had feelings for Shorty other than friendship? Oh, you men. You think if you show a little interest in a woman that every other man is to treat her like she was wearing your brand. Well, this woman is not wearing yours or anyone else's brand. What did you mean by, have you decided that I have branded you as mine as Linda remarked earlier," Theresa retorted angrily.

"Why, yes, fair lady if you will have me," Zack replied.

"You are sure of that? It seems that only a little while ago you were showing a lot of interest in the low cut blouse Linda was wearing," Theresa said.

"You at least did not run off and leave me. I hope to look beyond that high collar one of these days," Zack responded.

"Well, Mr. Zack Haney, you will not be looking beyond this high collar until I have a wedding ring on this finger," and she pointed. "Furthermore, who would want to marry a man that comes home shot up or possibly in a casket?"

Zack grinning, responded, "1 sure hope you do and has anyone ever told you that your eyes flash like sparklers when you are angry?"

"Zack Haney, you are impossible," Theresa remarked and she slowly moved into his arms once more.

"Zack, I do not believe that 1can live a life such as this. Never knowing where you are and worrying that you will be coming home like Shorty. Please give the ranger job up," Theresa pleaded.

"Theresa, I'11 wire my resignation to Captain Brock if it takes that for you. to marry me. This job is complete when those two bodies are on the way to Southwest Texas."

Tears began to collect in Theresa's eyes as she responded, "Oh, Zack, of course I'll marry you."

Chapter 13

Earlier as they had started out from the ranch, Alan and Lucinda had gotten into a bit of a confrontation about the religion that she planned to raise Amber under. Him being of the Mennonite faith, he was strongly opposed to the Catholic Church. Lucinda finally refused any compromise about it when Alan suggested they could discuss it another time.

"Alan, it is so silly of us to argue about this. After all, do we not all basically pray to one God?"

"Of course, you are right. Amber is your child and I should not have interfered at all," Alan responded.

"Alan, I need to go back to Amarillo and collect Amber. I miss her so much. So, if it is okay with you, I would like to leave tomorrow," Lucinda stated.

"Of course you miss her. Would you have any objection to my accompanying you on the train?" Alan asked.

"I should kiss you for allowing Amber to come. I am so happy and you know that I would not have the remotest objection to your joining me. It is wonderful that you want to come with me. I will feel so much safer riding the train to Amarillo. At that point, she related to him the story of how Zack had protected she and Theresa. You can meet Amber and my mother at the same time. But, I must warn you; Amber is a very precocious child," Lucinda said.

"Well, that will be okay with me. When we arrive in Amarillo, should I make two reservations for rooms at the Cattleman's Hotel for you and I?"

Alan inquired of her.

"It sounds lovely Alan, but I feel for the sake of propriety that I should stay at my mother's with Amber until we leave. I know that I have been a guest in your home for these many weeks but I believe you understand my hesitation,"

Lucinda replied.

"Lucinda, please do not concern yourself about it. I do fully understand.

I probably never should have introduced the subject. I, also hope that I have not offended you," was Alan's reply.

"Never. I know that you would never do anything to compromise me," Lucinda assured him.

"I believe that I should kiss you as an apology for my earlier interference," Alan remarked with a mischievous smile.

That is exactly what he did before she had a chance to agree or refuse.

Both adults were lost in the pleasures of each other. These two people are a great example that love is not just for the young, but also for the young at heart.

"Lucinda, I want us to continue to be as we are. Just enjoying being with each other and Amber. I want you both to feel that we can all be a very happy family," Alan said as he continued to embrace her.

"Alan, as long as 1have you and Amber, how could 1not be happy? As for Amber, I have no doubt that the two of you will be able to be very comfortable with one another. However, 1agree with you. I want us to get to know each other and especially that you are going to be able to cope with a five-year old child. You will be making the hardest adjustments, you see, I already love her dearly," Lucinda informed him.

"Well, now that we have our trip planned, maybe we should return to the ranch house and inform the others. Zack should be doing better in a day or two. Charlie and Milton will be here to help him and Theresa can run the ranch in our absence," Alan said with a pleased smile.

"I just hope that Zack and Theresa are able to get things straightened between them. Each of them certainly has a stubborn streak. I'm sure they both still need a little maturing. I am glad that you and 1 are able to talk so freely with one another," Alan added further.

"Alan, isn't that Milton and Linda coming from the ranch in the buckboard."

Alan asked with a chuckle in his voice, "You don't suppose Zack or Theresa sent someone to find us, do you?

"We shall know very shortly," Lucinda responded.

Coming to a stop, Alan waited for Milton to reach them.

"1 sure hate those two have to find out about this, this way, but it cannot be helped," Milton said to Linda.

Milton drew the buckboard to a stop as he came along side of the buggy.

"Morning, Mr. Haney, Miss Lucinda," Milton said.

"Milton, has something happened at the ranch? Are Zack and Theresa okay?" Alan inquired.

"Yes, sir, Zack and Theresa are okay, but Shorty has been mortally wounded. An escaped convict and his lady are to be shipped back to the sheriff in Waco. Zack is going to bring Shorty's body back here for burial in a few days." Milton informed him.

"Lucinda, it sounds as though we should have started back sooner." Alan commented.

"Mr. Haney, 1don't think that things would have ended any differently if the two of you had been there," Linda spoke for the first time.

"I do hope that Zack will give up his ranger job," Alan said worriedly.

"If Theresa has anything to do with it, you will not have to worry for much longer," Milton remarked.

"Milton, you and Linda go on into town. I hope that you can make the trip back here before too late. Be careful," Alan cautioned.

Back at the ranch house, Zack and Theresa have finally managed to be alone.

"Theresa, will you now, please come here and let me try to explain to you about Linda?" Zack asked.

"Really Zack, there is not anything to explain. I have known Linda for a long time and 1know that she loves the limelight. She puts on a good front, but she really is very harmless. Knowing that, I should never have allowed her to make me angry. I let her have her moment of glory at my expense.

Maybe Milton and she will someday make a commitment to one another. I think that Milton will try to hold out the longest," Theresa commented.

"You, my lovely one, need to come over here and sit beside me on the bed," Zack encouraged Theresa.

Theresa didn't need much encouragement. Slowly she walked to the side of Zack's bed. Zack reached out to her and pulled her down beside him. His hands explored her narrow waist. He could feel the warmth of her body through her cotton dress as well as her breast against his body.

Hearing someone enter the house and the stairs almost at the same time, Theresa quickly sat up, straightened her clothes and pushed her hair back in place. When Alan came rushing into the room, all was in place.

"Theresa, what has happened here today? Lucinda and I encountered Milton and Linda on our way back to the house. Zack, you are okay, aren't you?"

"Yes, he is fine. A little shaken, but at least he did not disturbs his wounds," Theresa answered Alan.

"Dad, I am fine. I can't say the same for poor Shorty. He had just come to the house this morning to tell me he had decided to return to Lamesa. I am having his body brought here for burial if that is okay with you. In the afternoon of that same day, Theresa and I will be married," Zack said as he gazed at his bride to be.

"Zack, who was the man that came here today and how on earth did Shortly get caught up in it?" Alan questioned.

"As I have just said, Shorty came to tell me he was leaving this morning.

This Tony Angelino had escaped from a state prison in Waco. His lady friend is the one that shot me from behind in Edmondson. Shorty apparently tried to stop him from coming into the house, but Tony kept yelling for me to come out. That it had to be him or me. Shorty's interference angered him, but it gave me time to get down the stairs and out to the corner of the house. Tony turned some of his ruthlessness on Shorty and shot him. Shorty didn't stand a chance against the likes of him," Zack explained.

"We need to send a wire to Shorty's family to let them know what has happened. If! were not laid up with these wounds, I could take him back home on the train," Zack added.

"Did I hear the word wedding just a few minutes ago?" Alan asked.

"You sure did," Zack said with a big smile on his face.

Lucinda came in the room just in time to hear Zack say he and Theresa were getting married. "That is wonderful news!" she exclaimed as she hugged her cousin.

"When do you two have this planned for? Lucinda asked.

"The preacher will be coming here in a few days to give Shorty a proper burial. Later that same day we will have the wedding," Zack said.

"A few days will be perfect timing," Alan stated.

"Lucinda and I will be leaving for Amarillo in the morning to collect her daughter Amber. I have a side trip planned for the Grand Canyon in Arizona, but we will be back before the wedding," Alan commented further.

"Dad, is there something that Lucinda and you are not telling us? It has been reported that the two of you have been seen leaving the ranch together a lot," Zack quizzed his dad.

"Well, Zack, Lucinda and I have discovered that love isn't just for the young. But we are not going to rush things. We have plenty of time," Alan remarked.

"Theresa, I am sorry that I will not be here to help get things ready, but we will be back in time for the wedding," Lucinda said with a genuine apology in her voice.

"Please, do not worry about that. Linda is here and more than happy to help with the preparations. You just worry about getting Amber here with you," Theresa remarked.

"If the two of you will excuse Lucinda and I, we have some packing to do for tomorrow's trip," Alan stated.

"Sure, you two go ahead," Theresa told them.

Alan said, "I'm sure glad things worked out for Zack and Theresa.

Theresa being Catholic and Zack Mennonite, I wasn't sure. It's lonesome for a man alone, I know since my wife died."

"I call Zack the " because he's always working our herd west of Plainview. He says he will take a herd to the Lubbock sale rather than Amari110. It's true that prices are higher there due to the lack of good beef in all that dry land. Folks need beef, the Army needs beef, and the Indian agents need beef. Now, with the train both ways, Amari110 auction bam or the Lubbock auction are accessible to the Bar-Six and I finally agreed to sell higher at Lubbock due to the easy way to move herds, I'm better off financially."

"The was right after all," Alan chuckled. "Maybe with the extra money, we both can afford a bride." Alan winked at Lucinda.

Lucinda blushed and said in a worried tone, "I'm Catholic, too. You are Mennonite and know that I will raise Amber as a Catholic."

Chapter 14

Alan and Lucinda arrived in Plainview early. This gave them plenty of time to purchase their train tickets for the trip to Amarillo.

"Lucinda, would you rather go to your mother's home without this old man?" Alan asked Lucinda.

"Stop it," Lucinda scolded. "You are not an old man. If you were that old, I could stay in the same hotel room with you without repercussions," she added.

The closer the train got to Amarillo, Alan could see Lucinda become more excited. *She is devoted to that child.* he thought.

The ride finally ended. Lucinda could hardly wait to see her daughter after all this time away from her. They had never been separated this long.

Alan quickly gathered their luggage and they walked a couple of blocks to the Cattleman's Hotel. Alan checked himself in and had his suitcase taken to his room.

Lucinda said, "My mother's house is only a short distance from here. It is within easy walking distance of the hotel."

"Then, let us be off," Alan quipped.

Amber must have been watching for her mother. As soon as she saw her coming inside the gate, she made an excited dash out of the door before her grandmother could stop her. She went flying into her mother's outstretched arms.

The reunion of mother and daughter nearly took Alan's breath away. He thought that he should never see such a beautiful scene again.

"Oh, Mommy, I knew you would come. I have missed you so much," Amber said as she clung to her mother.

Turning with Amber in her arms, Lucinda gave her mother a hug. "It is good to see you both again. Thank you, Mother."

"Mother, I would like for you to meet Mr. Alan Haney. He was good enough to accompany me on this trip to get Amber. Also, he is the one who employed Theresa."

"Pleased to meet you, ma'am," Alan said as he extended his hand.

"It is good to meet you, Mr. Haney," Mrs. Davis said. "Lucinda has written to us about you, your son Zack and your ranch."

"Mother, when we get back to Plainview, Theresa and Zack will be getting married. I will assume Theresa's duties while they are on their honeymoon. Amber will be accompanying me back to the ranch."

Amber looked up at this tall broad shouldered man with just a hint ofgray hair at his temples. "Are you going to be my new daddy? Are you in love with my mommy?" she blurted out.

"Honey, please," Lucinda said.

Alan said, "It is okay. You and I have just met Amber, but I have always wanted a daughter. So, while you are at the Bar-Six, you may call me Papa, Daddy or Mr. Alan. Whichever you like. May I call you my daughter, Amber?"

She giggled. "Sure, Dad, call me daughter."

Lucinda and Mrs. Davis did not know what to say.

Mrs. Davis changed the subject. "Mr. Haney, can I get you some coffee and maybe a piece of fresh peach pie to go with it?"

"That sounds good. I am always ready for pie and coffee," he said.

"Amber, have you ever been to or heard of the Grand Canyon?" Alan inquired.

"What is the Grand Canyon?" was Amber's response.

"Well, tomorrow we are going to take a train ride to Arizona where the Grand Canyon is. It is the largest and deepest natural canyon in the United States. Actually, it has been formed by many years of natural erosion of the earth by the Colorado River," Alan told her.

Chapter 15

Completing a four-hour train ride from Amarillo, Alan, Lucinda and Amber disembarked the train in Williams, Arizona.

Amber had decided that she liked Mr. Alan. That was the name she had decided to call him.

Much of the train ride from Amarillo, she occupied a seat between the two adults. She wanted to be near both of them.

Shortly after arriving at the Grand Canyon rim, a rider almost tumbled over the rim as he raced up to it before slowing his mount in hips down desperate slide to stop. The horse was a trembling gray mustang at the end.

The young man's face was as gray as his horse's mane.

Alan holding Amber's hand on one side, while Lucinda held the other, turned with Amber listening to the talk between the couple. "Did you see that young fool? He nearly killed himself and a beautiful Grula mustang," Alan fumed.

"Now, Alan," Lucinda remarked, "you sound as if the horse was more important than the man." She regretted her statement almost as soon as she had said it.

"Well, dang him anyway. The fool could have killed himself, but he had a choice. The horse had none," Alan stated.

Lucinda came back, "I know you are right and killing a beautiful capable horse would have been a great waste." Her eyes pleaded for forgiveness.

Alan leaned across the top of Amber's head and kissed Lucinda. Lucinda considered turning her cheek to receive the kiss, but decided she wouldn't risk Alan's ire. She returned his kiss fervently.

"Mommy, isn't kissing like that hot work? You look so red," Amber said and Lucinda blushed even a deeper red.

"Speaking of hot," Alan said, "why don't we go back to the cafe we passed on the way up here? We can get some cool water or lemonade."

So, the three of them headed back to the welcome shade of the cafe.

The young cowboy that abused his horse came into the cafe. "There is that fool who nearly killed his horse," Amber said a little too loudly.

The man jerked his head in the direction of Amber and bellowed. "Who are you calling a fool, little lady?" He then took two strides toward Amber.

Alan quickly stepped between the angry man and Amber. "You are that fool. You nearly killed an obviously well-trained cutting horse. Your next foolish mistake today was talking angrily to my stepdaughter." With this he carried a right cross to the man's chin. The cowboy was out cold before he hit the floor.

"Well, if you ladies are ready, we can head back into town and get ready to board our train back to Amarillo," Alan posed the question to Lucinda and Amber.

"Thank you, Alan, for a lovely day," Lucinda said as she dropped her head onto his shoulder and slept as the train moved along.

Lucinda and Amber returned to her mother's home when they arrived back in Amarillo. Alan kissed both mother and daughter good night and walked the short distance to the his hotel.

The next morning, Lucinda and Amber were packed and ready when Alan arrived for them. Amber was excited and could not be still.

The train pulled into the Plainview station around four o'clock that afternoon. Alan had wired ahead to Zack to have someone there to meet them.

Zack was waiting when they left the train.

"How have things been going at the ranch?" he asked his son.

"We have the cattle ready to bring into the rail yard next week. The Lubbock cattle sale will be the first leg of mine and Theresa's honeymoon," Zack responded.

Alan had been reluctant to change to the Lubbock cattle sale, but Zack had finally convinced him they would get a better price there because of the dry land conditions in that part of the state. Now the railroad made it easier to get the cattle to market.

"Well, now. Who is this pretty little miss?" Zack asked as he saw Amber.

"Zack, this is Lucinda's daughter Amber," Alan answered with a smile.

"My goodness, I do believe that it is getting cold," Lucinda exclaimed and gave a little shiver.

"I believe we are about to get one of those unseasonal cold fronts through here from Canada. I have some blankets here in the wagon for you," Zack responded.

"Theresa and 1have decided that we need to put the wedding off until next week," Zack added further.

"Zack, let's get this luggage loaded and try to get home before the sun goes down," Alan said.

The four of them reached the ranch house just as the sun was going down.

Theresa had come out on the veranda to welcome them back. As soon as the buggy stopped, Amber jumped down and ran to her cousin Theresa. "My goodness, it is so good to see you, Amber. Did you enjoy your train rides?"

Theresa enthused.

"Ladies, we need to get this luggage as well as you into the house. It is turning colder," Alan commented.

Theresa's room faced the north side of the ranch house. The cold air edged in around the wooden window frames.

Lucinda remembered lying in the warm embrace of her previous husband.

How she wished that she and Alan was having a wedding, not just Zack and Theresa.

Chapter 16

"Crash," came the sound of the stove door being closed. Lucinda, hearing the noise arose quietly so as not to awaken her sleeping child and went to the kitchen to investigate. She found Alan and Zack up feeding wood to the cook stove. Zack had just returned from the front veranda with an arm full of split wood. Alan had coffee brewing on the stove.

"It seems you men are as cold as we ladies," she said.

"Pshaw," Theresa said as she joined the group in the kitchen. "Men should be toughened to the cold . . . with all the hours they spend on horseback."

Theresa smiled that engaging smile that warmed Zack's heart.

"Sweet lady. Just the sight of you warms my heart," he offered.

"Well, I'm still cold. Don't engaged folks deserve a buntling blanket and shared body warmth on a bed?" Theresa asked.

Zack's knees went weak. *Did Theresa just say that she wants to be in bed with me?* Zack asked himself.

"A husband in the bed can sure keep a wife warm," Lucinda replied. She smiled a coquettish smile at Alan.

"Pshaw," Alan responded. "I miss sleeping with my now deceased wife," a look of sadness filled his face.

"Alan, as chaperone, I can give permission for such cOUl1ing, can't IT' asked Lucinda.

"Yes, certainly," assured Alan. "If you two can promise to stay chaste until after the wedding, I think that it is a warm idea!" Alan agreed.

Buntling blankets have been used since colonial times.

He then went on, "Lucinda, may I have formal permission to court you as of tonight? I am thinking of sharing a bed with you and Amber tonight, too."

"Well, yes, Mr. Haney, your courtship is acceptable to me," Lucinda replied.

"Besides, if someone does not keep me warm, how can I stay alert for my chaperoning duties?" Lucinda tacked on. "Plus, Amber is there to chaperone us!"

"Did you just give me permission to sleep with you, too?" Alan asked with excitement in his voice.

"Yes, but do not be trying anything to come across that rolled blanket since Amber will be in bed with us," Lucinda remarked lightly.

The couples took their coffee cups to the stove and filled them. Standing too close to the hot metal, Theresa's sleeping gown smelled hot and may have burst into flames, but friends pulled her back from the hot cast iron stove.

"You and Zack better go on and share some covers on one bed before you catch on fire," Lucinda ordered.

Alan said, "Zack get all the covers of f your bed and put them on Theresa's bed."

"Well, Mr. Haney, are you going to do the same courtesy to me? 1 need some extra blankets, too." Lucinda smiled.

Alan was still in sock feet but he nearly tripped as Zack slid into his boots.

Zack had pulled on his boots for retrieving an armload of wood.

"Dam, you would think that 1was as excited as a young buck like Zack."

Alan laughed heartily.

Lucinda remarked, "Well, I think that God's hand is in this, the timing of the storm. It seems to have speeded up a courtship that 1had been hoping for."

Before another ten months, new sleeping arrangements would be accomplished.

"Zack, do you believe the boldness of my response toward your dad?"

"Alan, was I too bold?" Lucinda asked sincerely. "1 don't want you to think that I'm a loose woman."

"I do not think that," Alan responded

Lucinda giggled and Alan laughed a hearty man's laugh.

That night, in the next room over, Theresa said to Zack, "Do you believe the noise and laughter coming from those two people?" She giggled herself.

"Look whose being noisy," Zack responded, then threw his warm arm over the buntling blanket and around Theresa, pulling her close under the blankets.

Alan also had put his arm over Lucinda and Amber, hugging them close.

"1 think I am in love with you already at the start of this courtship. What will develop later?"

"We'll see," Lucinda responded and cuddled closer to Alan. She could feel the heat of his powerful body radiating under the covers piled on them.

Lucinda groaned a satisfied moan.

"It sure is quiet next door, now," Theresa said to Zack. "What are they up to? Do think we need to check on them?" she quipped.

"Forget it," Zack responded. "They are the chaperones. Surely they know how to behave with Amber chaperoning them." Zack smiled in the darkness but tightened his hold on Theresa. "If you turn your back to me, 1 can get closer to you," Zack remarked.

"How do you know so much about keeping a girl warm?" Theresa asked.

"Well, keeping warm seems to come naturally to me," Zack said into her hair.

Theresa felt the warm pocket of air spread under all those covers. She turned over and pushed back against the rolled up blanket. "I can't wait until our wedding night when we can get rid of this buntling blanket keeping us apart." Theresa then blushed in the darkness at how bold she must have sounded.

Just before dawn Alan slid out of bed to pull his boots on. Lucinda roused,

"Where are you going, Alan?"

"Alan, where is 'Mr. Haney'?" he joked. "Sleep with an employee and they get bold with using your first name," Alan joked on.

"I am going to get some more wood in to heat up the kitchen stove," Alan said.

Lucinda responded, "Employee? I'm being courted and 1 plan to call you

Alan, so get used to it!" she laughed.

When Alan reached the kitchen, Zack was already piling wood into the cook stove.

Alan asked, "Didn't you save any work for me?'

"Yes, Dad, you can bring in some wood for the pot bellied stove in the den," Zack answered.

"This has been a terrible night," Alan teased. "First my housekeeper started calling me by my first name and then my son starts dishing out the ranch chores!" Alan smiled.

"Well, Dad, you asked me and I responded. You slept with Lucinda and giggled half of the night," Zack stated.

"Half the night?" Alan came back. "Well, 1was kept awake the other half by giggling from the office bedroom of Theresa's," he came back.

"Do I see Lucinda being my stepmother?" Zack grinned.

"Slow down, son, we will see what the future holds," Alan remarked.

Chapter 17

The weather had warmed back up and Reverend West had arrived for the burial of Shorty. It seemed only fitting that a happy occasion should follow this sad one.

Zack picked a yellow rose from the vase of roses on the dining room table, placed in it in his lapel, then turned and walked over to the oak tree where

Reverend West waited. This was his big day. In just a few hours, he and Theresa would be Mr. and Mrs. Zack Haney. It had a nice ring to it.

He had been trying all day to see Theresa, but was thwarted at every attempt. Everyone kept telling him it was bad luck for the bride and groom to see each other before the ceremony on their wedding day. Bad luck, he certainly did not want to risk that. These last few days had seemed to last forever.

The wedding march began and Zack turned to see Amber coming down the grassy aisle dropping rose petals. Next, Linda appeared and came to stand at her place as Theresa's maid-of—honor. Milton had taken his position as best man beside Zack. Then the one person Zack had been waiting for all day came down the carpet of grass on the arm of Alan. Zack's soon-to-be bride was a vision of white purity as she came to rest at his side.

The ceremony soon got underway. Reverend West said, "Zack, do you take this woman, Theresa Mendoza, to be your lawfully wedded wife? Zack's response of yes had no sounds of hesitation. Theresa Mendoza, do you take Issac 'Zack' Haney to be your lawfully wedded husband?"

Her voice was crystal clear as she said yes.

Reverend West held his Bible in his right hand up to the sky in prayer.

Then looking back at the happy young couple, he said to Zack, "Place the ring on Theresa's hand and repeat after me. With this ring I thee wed for richer, for poorer, in sickness and in health. Now, Theresa, place the ring on Zack's finger and repeat after me."

After the exchanging of the vows and rings, Reverend West said, "I now pronounce you man and wife. You may now kiss the bride."

Zack was thinking he would never get to this part. Taking Theresa in his arms, he again tasted the sweetness of her lips.

Reverend West cleared his throat softly and the happy couple stepped apart. Turning the couple to face the assembled crowd, Reverend West said, "Let me introduce Mr. and Mrs. Zack Haney."

As soon as Theresa had said "I do," Linda handed her back the bridal bouquet of yellow roses. Applause thundered from the cowboys gathered for the happy occasion.

Milton had moved over to stand by Linda and had placed his hand around her waist, pulling her closer, he whispered, "I'll consider such a union with you later."

Linda, however, wondered if she would always be the bridesmaid and never the bride, as she blinked back tears. But she was truly happy for Zack and Theresa.

Before Theresa threw her bridal bouquet, she searched the crowd for her cousin Lucinda. It is said that the one who catches the bridal bouquet will marry shortly.

Bringing Lucinda a cup of lemonade, Alan said, "Well, it would appear that I have just lost my housekeeper and bookkeeper for a while. Lucinda, I hope that you are seriously considering filling the vacancy temporarily?"

"You just try giving that job to someone else, no matter how long or short a time the job is, Alan, or do I call you Mr. Haney?"

Theresa, spotting Lucinda, turned her back and tossed her bridal bouquet into the air and into Lucinda's outstretched hands. Turning back to the crowded, she laughed and clapped loudly at seeing she had hit her mark.

Lucinda, too laughing gaily, took Alan's arm and hugged it saying, "Please sit and visit with me a minute," as she locked her hazel eyes on his blue ones.

Alan too had turned his eyes from the bride and groom to study the maturer woman at his side. At thirty-three Lucinda still looked to be in her twenties.

Zack and Theresa had slipped away from the crowd. Taking her in his arms, he was finally able to let his senses enjoy the feel of his beautiful new bride.

Theresa whispered, "Zack, as badly as I hate to interrupt this heavenly experience, we need to make our way into Plainview to the hotel. Tomorrow your job as a fulltime cowboy will begin again when we reach Lubbock.

"Fulltime cowboy? That doesn't leave much time to get to know that sof t, shapely body of yours, Mrs. Haney, so I better get you into Plainview, sol can remedy that problem. I have had promises of learning what is beneath those high collars that you have insisted upon wearing since you have been here. So my love, your chariot awaits you."

Theresa snuggled closely to Zack on the buggy seat and looking dreamily at her new husband said, "Those high-necked collars are definitely gone, my "High Plains Cowboy."